Also by Neil Davies

Novella

The Demon Guardian

Novelette

The Vampire Worms

EMILY IN THE WALL
Twelve Chilling Tales of Horror and Suspense

EMILY IN THE WALL

Twelve Chilling Tales of Horror and Suspense

Neil Davies

A
Grinning Skull Press
Publication

DEDICATION

This collection is dedicated to Cathy, Jonathan, and Rhianne, who keep me going day after day.

Table of Contents

The Ten-Year Anniversary

Harry Dixon was a hero. He was a survivor of the British Army's defeat at the hands of Zulu warriors at *Isandlwana*, feted alongside the heroes of *Rorke's Drift* as a true British hero of the Zulu War.

And it was a lie.

January 22nd, 1879.

A date that burned fiercely in his memory. *Was it really ten years ago? That awful battle? That slaughter?*

It did not seem so to Harry Dixon. Almost every night, he woke in the dark, sweating, crying out in fear as ethereal Zulu warriors attacked him with their *assegais.*

And it did not seem so on the dull, overcast morning of the ten-year anniversary.

An exhausted Harry carefully shaved with cold, soapy water and a near-blunt cutthroat razor. The stubble of the night was scraped away, and for a moment, he stared at himself in the small shaving mirror. The mustache held flecks of gray, as did his thinning hair. His face was creased, his forehead heavy with frown lines. His eyes were dull.

He could not remember the details of that day so long ago. Only a blurred memory of the terrifying attack by the Zulus, and then his stumbling into *Rorke's Drift* later that same day. What actually happened during the battle, how he had managed to fight off the Zulu and escape the slaughter of his fellow soldiers, he could not remember.

They called him a hero because he had survived. But a nagging guilt at the back of his mind told him there was nothing heroic about *how* he survived. He wished he could remember, even though he feared what had remained hidden for ten years.

* * *

On leaving his lodgings, and with the London stone beneath his feet forming a solid and, more importantly, safe foundation, he grew more sure of himself. The background noise of the city, horses' hooves on cobblestones, street vendors' cries, all helped to drown out the doubt and guilt in his mind. Yet he wondered, as he did every year, whether this would be the reunion where his supposed heroism would finally be revealed for the lie he felt it surely was. Someone would know the truth. Or perhaps *he* would finally remember. And if he did, would he reveal his own guilt to that assembly of *true* heroes? Or would he continue to hide, to play the part that the newspapers had placed on him even before his return to England?

Up ahead, a typical London fog was drifting into the

streets, dropping a gray shroud over the people, the buildings.

What's that?

The background noise had changed, taking on the rhythmic pulse of a Zulu chant. Voices rose. Shields of animal hide were slammed with *assegais* in perfect synchronization, each beat driving into his heart, his belly. He could almost see them, running over the hills, a black wave of power and death.

Fear squeezed his chest. Sweat blossomed on his face. How could he escape? Where could he hide? Where could he run to?

This time.

The thought brought reality sweeping back. He was in the city once more, with city sounds and city sights. No Zulu chants. No attacking army of warriors.

I ran while my fellow soldiers fought and died.

He was certain of it, the guilt heavy in his stomach. How could he go through with this reunion when, other than his *being* at *Isandlwana*, his story was a lie?

The same sounds of the city that he had found so reassuring now seemed to crowd in on him, rising in volume, making other thoughts almost impossible. Streets that had seemed almost empty now buzzed with people, talking, shouting, pushing!

He needed to get away, to escape. A place to be on his own. To think.

Trying to return to his lodgings, he found the way blocked by phantom shapes that swirled and darted in the growing fog. They may have been people. They may have been ghosts. He could not tell.

There was an alley opposite. He ducked inside and sat in its deep shadow, his breath blowing heavy, his nerves straining, ready to snap.

Why don't they all go away? What do they want of me?

* * *

He could never understand why they had not formed a *laager* when they camped in the shadow of the sphinx-like hill, *Isandlwana*. The circling of wagons had been standard procedure on similar expeditions in the past, but apparently, the order had come from Lord Chelmsford himself. There was no arguing with that. Chelmsford knew what he was doing. He presumably had his reasons. But it was an oversight that worried Harry Dixon and some of the other soldiers around him.

Chelmsford surprised them again, later, when he rode out of the camp with, it seemed, a good half of the men. He left behind soldiers of the 1st Battalion, including Harry himself, and some of the 2nd. There were others, too, mostly a native contingent. The talk was that Chelmsford was off to crush the Zulus, and that was fine by Harry. He had no particular wish to face the enemy. Not that he doubted the superiority of the British soldier, with his Martini-Henry rifle and his training. But the natives frightened him. The Zulus were rumored to be fierce fighters.

He wished Chelmsford every success. He wanted to go home in one piece.

"You think his Lordship is doing the right thing?" said Sid Morehouse, a friend from the parade ground back home.

"I *hope* His Lordship is doing the right thing," said Harry. "Otherwise, we're all in trouble."

Sid nodded and wiped sweat from his forehead.

"I can understand why the natives go about with next to no clothes on most of the time," he said. "Far too bloomin' hot in this country."

"Makes you nostalgic for a bit of London fog or good old English rain," said Harry.

"Pulleine's been left in charge," said Sid, lowering his voice to a whisper. "Does that make sense to you?"

"He's a Lieutenant Colonel," said Harry. "Don't suppose Chelmsford could ignore him in the chain of command."

"But Pulleine! He's a pen pusher. He doesn't know how to command troops in the field."

"He won't need to, will he," said Harry. "Chelmsford will break the Zulus, and we won't have to do anything."

"Do you really believe that?"

Harry looked across the bustling camp, British and native soldiers, some civilians tagging along, wagons haphazardly strewn about. He *had* to believe that they would not be attacked. He was scared just being in Zululand. Anything more was too terrifying to contemplate.

* * *

"Harry? Are you okay?"

Harry, still crouched in the shadows of the alley, looked up and, for a moment, failed to recognize the speaker who stood nearby. He looked closer.

"Sid? Sid Morehouse?"

"Yes, Harry, it's Sid," said the figure, moving closer. "I saw you duck into the alley here, but I wasn't sure it was you at first. Why are you hiding in here?"

"I get a bit jumpy," said Harry, grateful to talk to someone who could understand. "Don't go out much these days."

"Do you still have nightmares?"

"Yes, almost every night."

"Me, too," said Sid. "Sometimes, it seems like my whole life is a dream, a nightmare."

"It doesn't go away," said Harry. "I don't remember that much, but the images…the Zulus attacking…men dying…"

"It's okay," said Sid. "I understand, Harry. I'm the same myself. It never goes away."

The two old comrades fell silent. Sid slid to the alley floor alongside Harry.

"You going to the reunion?" said Harry after some time.

"I don't think so," said Sid. "It's mostly the lads from *Rorke's Drift*. You were there, though. You going?"

"Probably," said Harry, growing thoughtful. "Now that you mention it, I don't remember seeing you at *Rorke's Drift*, Sid. Where did you go after you escaped *Isandlwana*?"

"Harry," said Sid as a sudden gust of wind swirled dust into the air of the alley, into Harry's eyes, forcing him to close them for a moment. "Whoever said I escaped?"

Harry opened his eyes, rubbing the grit from them, and turned to ask Sid what he meant. But Sid was no longer there. Harry was, once again, alone in the alley.

He shivered, knowing that Sid could not have left without him knowing, without him hearing something. A cold finger of fear ran the length of his spine and tickled the base of his neck. He thought he heard a distant sound of Zulu drumming.

Harry Dixon, as much as he shunned the companionship of his fellow man, felt a sudden urge to be among them once again. He did not want to be alone in a dark alley. He pushed to his feet and almost ran into the street. It was not busy, but there were some people about, enough to help him regain a semblance of control.

Sid Morehouse was nowhere to be seen. Harry was not surprised.

* * *

When the attack came, Harry and Sid fought alongside each other.

Lieutenant Colonel Pulleine organized his defense as best he could, faced with the unexpected full force of the Zulu army of over twenty thousand well-organized warriors. Slowly, the British line was forced back, closer in to the camp. The Zulu attack formation, the traditional *horns and chest of the buffalo*, stretched the British defense, with the right-hand side finally giving way. Zulu warriors swarmed into the camp, and the hand-to-hand battle was joined.

The chants and calls of the attacking warriors mingled with the screams of the dying and the clatter of gunfire. Gun smoke from the Martini-Henry rifles drifted across the battlefield, clouds of desperation and despair. Swords clashed with *assegais*. Hands grappled hands. Men died on both sides, but as the battle progressed, more and more red-uniformed bodies littered the ground.

Harry and Sid had been forced back, toward the rear of the camp. They stood back to back, surrounded. With no ammunition left, they used their rifles as clubs, beating back Zulu warriors with desperate swings. *Assegais* stabbed toward them, never quite reaching the two bloodied, sweat- and grime-covered British soldiers. The rifles grew heavier with each swing, the heat more overpowering. Harry felt dizzy, disoriented. He dropped his rifle.

An *assegai* found his side, ground into it. Through the white-hot pain, he could feel it inching further in, then suddenly pull back. The pain burst in sharp, jagged lines from the wound, spreading throughout his body. A terrible weakness accompanied it, making his hands shake and his legs tremble.

He saw, through bleary eyes, a Zulu warrior lunging toward him. By instinct, he grabbed at a surprised Sid and pulled him across. The *assegai* plunged deep into Sid's stomach.

As he fell, Sid looked up at Harry. He could not speak through the blood already bubbling from his lips, but the eyes were full of shock, of questions.

Harry could only stare in silence. He had no answers, no excuse other than fear and cowardice. As Sid's body twitched, already more dead than alive, despair and disgust battled with a tenuous sanity in Harry's mind. Had he sunk so low that he would betray a friend? *Murder* a friend? For although the Zulu warrior's *assegai* had struck the blow, Harry had no illusions of who was to blame.

He continued to stare as Sid's eyes glazed over, the last threads of life drifting away. In a moment of brutal clarity, Harry knew that the betrayal had been ultimately worthless. What had he gained by avoiding one *assegai* when so many more waited to kill him? His soul was surely damned to an eternity in Hell. There seemed no point in delaying its journey. He gathered what little courage he had left.

"Come on then!" he screamed, closing his eyes, waiting. "Just do it. Get it over with."

But no thrust came. No killing blows.

Cautiously, he opened his eyes.

The sky had darkened, a shadow falling across the battle-field. It was 2:29 p.m., and the solar eclipse brought premature night to the bloody camp.

For one moment, Harry hoped the Zulu warriors would be frightened by the sudden darkness, perhaps even run away. But they did no more than the remaining British soldiers. They looked at the sky. They continued to fight.

Perhaps that small delay was all that Harry needed?

He was about to run when a Zulu stepped in front of him. But this was no warrior.

A *Sangoma* stood before him, goat bladder tied at the back of the hair, a belt of snake skin around his waist. He flicked a cow-tail whisk and pointed at Harry.

Witch doctor, thought Harry. *Why don't they just kill me?*

The *Sangoma* spat words at him in Zulu, chanted and danced around him while the warriors stood and watched. He thought he saw pity in some of their stares.

He made a break for it. *Assegais* were raised, but a shout from the *Sangoma* froze them in place. Harry was not stopped as he ran from the battlefield, chased by the darkness as the sun reappeared in the sky.

*** * ***

"You really believe a Zulu Witch Doctor put a curse on you?" said Sid, as Harry finally stumbled his way back into his lodgings.

Harry stopped, dropping his keys onto the threadbare carpet. His army colleague stood by the small window, the light seeming to almost pass through him, illuminating him from within.

"You're dead," said Harry, his voice breaking. "I saw you die at *Isandlwana*."

"I may be dead," said Sid. "But you're the one who thinks he's cursed."

"I can't be talking to you," said Harry as he sat in a chair and covered his face with his hands. "It's not real. I'm going mad."

"Speaking of *mad*," said Sid. "I wasn't exactly pleased when you killed me!"

The shock of the accusation stung Harry into pulling his hands from his face.

"The Zulus killed you."

"You used me as a shield so they killed me instead of you."

The truth weighed heavily, and Harry hung his head in shame.

"I was scared. I didn't think."

"I'm not here for an apology," said Sid, still standing at the window, never moving. "Nor am I here for revenge. It's been ten years, Harry. The Zulu Nation is gone, its people scattered. You weren't cursed by the Witch Doctor. You were cursed by your own guilt."

"The nightmares," said Harry, groaning. "Every night, the nightmares."

"You were meant to die that day, just as I did. But the Witch Doctor interfered after I was killed and decided it would be more cruel to let you live with your memories rather than simply die at the point of a spear."

"Ten years," said Harry. "Ten years of being frightened to go to sleep."

"You're so tired you're seeing things, hearing things."

"Like the drums, the warriors. And you!"

Harry, still staring at the carpet, waited for a response. Silence. Slowly, he looked up toward the window. For a moment, he thought he saw a figure standing there, but it was just the sunlight, the curtains, and shadows. He was alone.

He hung his head back down and cried.

"Surely ten years is enough suffering for one man," he said through his sobs.

In the distance, he could hear the drums, the chanting, the banging of *assegais* on shields.

He stood and turned.

Where there should have been a wall, there now stretched the open plains of Zululand. Some distance behind him rose *Isandlwana*, where the bodies of his fellow soldiers lay, cut open by the Zulu warriors so their spirits might be free. Against the bright sky, the hill gave no clue as to the bloody battle that had been fought there, the battle Harry had run from.

He turned again as the rhythmic banging and chanting rose in volume, becoming almost deafening.

A dust cloud on the horizon hardened into thousands of Zulu warriors, charging toward him. Already the flanks were moving out into the classic pincer formation. If he did not move quickly, the *horns of the Buffalo* would close around him, and he would be trapped.

Chelmsford was a fool to underestimate the Zulus.

Harry knew that now, ten years on.

He ran, away from *Isandlwana* and toward *Rorke's Drift*, where he might be safe, because the battle at *Rorke's Drift* was a victory for the British. The soldiers stationed at *Rorke's Drift* were heroes. He was a hero, too, because he threw his friend on a spear to save himself and then ran away. As he ran now.

The warriors were closing. Soon they would be within throwing distance, and Harry tensed himself, ready for an *assegai* to hit him in the back. It never came, but the battle cries of the warriors did. Loud. Deafening.

Other sounds intruded. Puzzling, out-of-place sounds. Running footsteps on wood. People talking as though nothing was happening, as though it was just another day.

He risked a glance back. The warriors were closer again. He could see their enraged faces, the *assegais* raised, ready to strike. They were angry he had evaded them for ten years. But now they could finally kill him.

He ran. He heard a horse, a shout, but could only see the

African plains and the onrushing Zulus.

* * *

"He ran right out into the road, he did," said the cab driver, red-faced, flustered.

The Police Constable nodded and wrote everything down in his notebook. "And I suppose you would have had no chance of stopping," said the Constable, without looking up from his notes.

"The horse was on him before I realized it," said the cab driver. "The beast panicked, pulled the cab on. I could feel the wheels bump over him, I could." He shuddered at the memory.

The Constable looked at the twisted, bloodied body of Harry Dixon and could see the wheel marks across his broken head, running down his body. Somehow, the wheel had sliced him open. His guts leaked from the wound.

"Poor man just wasn't looking," he said. "I don't think there's any doubt that this was a tragic accident."

"I wonder who he was?" said the cab driver.

The Constable shrugged. It did not seem to matter.

And if anyone heard the faint sound of drums, of chanting, of *assegais* clattering against shields in the distance, they did not say anything. Nor did they speak if they heard a distant cry for help, as though from a disembodied spirit, carried away by those who had liberated it.

Ten years of nightmares were over. An eternity lay ahead.

Candy Lady

Dennis Wells watched the Candy Lady walk the wet sand of Point Clear.

It took him several long, frustrating seconds to get the focus on the binoculars just right, and for a moment, he was worried he had lost her, but she wasn't difficult to find again, her bright pink skirt a beacon at the water's edge. And as he watched her, following her every move in magnified close-up, he knew he had a problem. She was becoming more than just an anonymous victim, more than just the bait in another of his many traps; she was becoming a *person,* and he was falling in love with her. His Candy Lady.

* * *

She had arrived in the Stalking Ground just two days ago, alone and with nothing but her handbag and a small over-night case. From where he sat, outside the Coach House Café at Brightlingsea Harbor watching the raspberry sorbet in his hand slowly melting in the sun, she was impossible to ignore. The pink skirt, tight around the hips, gently flaring out to flap around her legs just below the knee, the same skirt that made her so easy to spot through the dubious focus of the binoculars, brought life and color to the otherwise gray and faintly shabby surroundings of the typical Essex town. The pink skirt, the pink sorbet, memories of brightly colored sweet jars… He named her Candy Lady there and then.

He was distracted by shuffling at a nearby table and watched a man in his early thirties lean forward, the delicate, almost feminine contours of his face anachronistic above the gym- and steroid-developed muscles displayed by the sleeveless t-shirt he wore. The face remained impassive, but the body language was clear. Grant Heddison, Dennis's reason for being in the South of England, had also seen Candy Lady and was equally captivated by her. That should be good; it meant everything was in place and the plan could progress. Nevertheless, his stomach knotted uncharacteristically, and he felt a fluttering of uncertainty.

The Candy Lady, oblivious to the attention of the two men nearby, moved off at a stroll toward the far side of the harbor. Dennis followed. He did not look back at Heddison, understanding the man's pattern well enough to know there was no immediate threat and he was safe to concentrate on the woman ahead of him.

She was perfect. Not too tall, just over five foot, not too skinny, blonde, late twenties to early thirties. If he had designed the perfect bait for his trap, it would have looked just like her. In truth, he *had* designed it, on paper, scanned into the computer, digitized, 3D, lifelike, but even he hadn't thought of the almost fluorescent pink skirt, the bright blue top. She was *more* than perfect. The unfamiliar knot in his stomach was so tight he felt physically sick.

She walked up the steps and into the concrete complex of stylish apartments overlooking the marina. He watched her enter one of the buildings, dropped the remains of his un-eaten, melted cone into a nearby bin, wiped his sticky hand on his jeans, and walked into the nearby public toilets, where he locked himself into a cubicle and masturbated. She really was *that* perfect.

* * *

Over on Point Clear, a family had drifted close to where his Candy Lady stood watching the gray North Sea advancing slowly over sand still wet from the last high tide. For a mo-ment, the daughter of the family pulled his attention away with her long legs, denim shorts, and far-too-tight t-shirt, but she was too young, probably still in her teens, and bru-nette. She was not perfect enough to persuade Heddison to change his target. Even so, the family group was getting too close and could interfere, and there was a part of his mind that wished they would. For the first time that day, he began to sweat.

* * *

The day after her arrival, he had waited, drinking tea at

Triscini's wine and coffee bar on the edge of the residential site, until she pushed her way through the double doors of her apartment block. Her choice of clothing was slightly disappointing, black leggings and a green t-shirt, but everything else about her was just as he remembered, just as he had dreamed about in the night.

He was thankful that Grant Heddison, true to his form, had stayed away to prepare. He suppressed a pang of guilt. He should have been watching Heddison, not the woman, but he was confused and driven by his need to see her again. It went against his professional judgment. He was helpless before these strange feelings and compulsions.

Once again, it was easy to follow as she spent an hour or so around the harbor, treating herself to a cone of chips from the Waterside Café, sitting on a bench in front of the yacht club to eat them while watching small pleasure boats drift back and forth on the placid water. After throwing the empty paper cone into a bin, she headed for the bus stop, and he stopped following. The boundaries of the Stalking Ground were very strict, and she was about to travel beyond them. He dare not stray too far from Heddison.

It was easy to scoop the paper cone out of the waste bin, and he once again utilized the cubicle in the public toilets. This time, masturbating into the paper cone her fingers had plucked chips from added an extra *frisson* that made his orgasm even stronger. Afterward, he felt exhausted, drained, and confused. Could he abandon his months of planning, his careful trailing of the volatile Grant Heddison, all for a woman he barely knew?

* * *

The third day, today, he had once again waited alone at Triscini's. This time his Candy Lady did not disappoint. She was wearing the same pink skirt as on the first day but with a different, purple, t-shirt. He was excited, nervous, his knotted stomach twisting harder than ever as she made to walk toward the harbor and then changed her mind, heading for the wine bar where he sat.

She took a table one over from his and smiled as the waitress took her order for black coffee. He fought hard not to stare while also struggling with the compulsion to run. She was too close. He felt the blood rushing to his cheeks.

"Excuse me?"

For a moment, he did not react to the soft voice, frozen in his seat, hoping she was talking to a returning waitress.

"Sorry to interrupt you, but I wondered if you knew the times of the ferry to Point Clear?"

A short, frantic turn of the head confirmed the worst. There was no one else. She was talking to him.

He felt sick, and his voice broke as he tried to reply. He coughed, forced a smile. How could she affect him this way? He tried to speak again. "I think they run about every fifteen minutes or so. I'm only visiting, so I'm not too sure. Sorry."

She returned his smile, and the knot in his stomach unraveled and twisted again tighter than ever.

"Sorry, I thought you lived around here."

"No problem." Why was he still talking? She had ended the conversation; he had a perfect escape route, and yet he could not stop himself. "I'm a collector, down here on business."

To his surprise, she showed a genuine interest.

"Anything rare?"

"Probably not, although some earlier pieces from the collection did make it into the national papers."

"Really? I only work in an office. I wish I had an interesting job like yours."

He smiled but said nothing more as she finished her coffee, left the money on the table, and rose from her seat.

"Well, thank you for your help…" She raised an inquisitive eyebrow.

"Dennis," he said, quickly, immediately cursing himself for using his real name.

"Dennis." She smiled. "I'm Andrea. I'd love to chat a bit longer, but I've promised myself I'd get over to Point Clear early today. Maybe we could meet later?"

"Yes, I'd like that," and to his surprise, he found he would, although he knew it was not likely to be under pleasant circumstances. He felt sad about that, disappointed, and that scared him more than anything else.

He watched her walk away, turning her head once to smile back at him. As he returned the smile, he saw Heddison leaning against the nearby railings, looking out over the moored boats but only truly seeing the Candy Lady. His hand trembled as he signaled for the waitress to bring his bill. He had told the truth; he *was* a collector, but was he willing to pay the full price this time?

He paid for his tea and was not surprised when he looked

up again to see that Heddison had gone, no doubt having overheard the short conversation. He would be heading for his van. Dennis took a deep breath to steady himself and, picking up the binoculars' case from by his feet, walked un-hurriedly to the nearest semi-circular viewing platform built as part of the new apartment complex. He simply needed to treat this like any other business deal and not get personally involved. He had already risked too much by changing his plans.

He pulled the binoculars from their case and stood at the railings, the marina spreading before him and, directly oppo-site, Point Clear, barely rising out of the water, empty sand and sparse grass, a café and an amusement arcade out of sight over the slight swell of the land. Behind, apartment balconies overlooked him, but he ignored them. He was just another tourist enjoying the view. Nothing suspicious.

He turned first toward the floating quayside to his left, finding his Candy Lady stepping carefully past the parents and children crab fishing off the edge. He could see the top of the small flat-bottomed boat that was the foot ferry, but there were too many people for him to see her actually board the boat. For a short while, he scanned back and forth, wor-ried she might have changed her mind, but after five minutes, when the ferry left the quayside, his Candy Lady was the only passenger.

* * *

He relaxed a little as the family moved away, heading

back toward the café and amusements, leaving Candy Lady alone once more on the sand. And now came the silver van with perfect timing, driving slowly down onto the sand, the family stepping to one side to let it through. It was not uncommon. Cars often parked near the water's edge, their occupants looking out to sea, not caring to step outside and brave the typically changeable British weather. No one would pay much attention to a silver van being driven slowly and carefully on the sands of Point Clear. No one but him. But then, he'd been waiting for this.

He was shifting his weight nervously from foot to foot, but it was not possible to stay still while watching the drama unfold. He knew what was coming, had witnessed similar scenes many times before, but for the first time, he fought the feeling that he should do something, be there to protect his Candy Lady.

Andrea. He was unsure whether he had ever known the name of a victim, at least not before the event. Once it made the papers, he would see the name, read about the family, but it never felt important. It never made them any more *real! Andrea.* It was uncomfortable, unsettling, and he struggled to hold the binoculars steady, his hands trembling, his stomach convulsing, cramping. He did not know what to do. It was an unfamiliar and unwelcome feeling.

The silver van crept closer to her as she walked, unaware, along the water's edge. He concentrated on the technique, striving to be clinical, professional, as the van stopped and Heddison, with adrenaline-fueled speed, leaped from the driver's seat.

She struggled. Her legs kicked out from under the pink skirt; she clawed at the large arm around her throat. Through the binoculars, he was able to see the whole thing up close, see the fear, the panic in her eyes, and the ease with which Heddison threw her into the back of the van. It was as smooth and professional an abduction as he had ever seen, but he felt light-headed and nauseous. The impressive demonstration of technique did not, for once, bring forth admiration for the perpetrator but anger and hatred and fear for the victim.

He had to do something. He could not allow this to continue to its natural and, before now, desired conclusion. It risked everything he had planned for, but he could not leave his Candy Lady, Andrea, to her fate. The thought made him sick.

He hurried, pushing the binoculars into their case as he ran back toward the harbor and his car. Heddison worked fast. He could not afford to delay.

* * *

The engine started the first time despite the shake in his hand as he turned the key. He crashed the gears finding first, began to pull away from the curb, and slammed his foot on the brake. A tractor. A *fucking tractor* towing a small boat down toward the receding tide, blocking him in as it maneuvered its way through the narrow street.

He slammed the steering wheel in frustration, the unfamiliar sting of tears in his eyes. Everything was wrong about this; everything was strange and unsettling and *wrong*! He was a professional. He had never experienced any difficulties before, and he had pursued many like Heddison in his life. But he had never seen a victim like the Candy Lady before, *his* Candy Lady, his Andrea.

He refused to dwell on thoughts of where Heddison might be right now, how far along his set, almost religious ritual would have proceeded, how much fear and panic and agony Andrea might be experiencing. He could not bear to think of that.

With deliberate and cruel slowness, the tractor pulled its load between the parked cars and curious bystanders while Dennis edged his car inch by inch toward freedom. The moment he felt the gap was there, he pushed the accelerator and twisted the wheel and was out, catching the bow of the towed boat a glancing blow, cracking the glass of his headlight and showering splinters from the damaged hull, bringing cries of surprise and some anger from those standing nearby. He did not care; even if anyone noted the registration number of his car, he did not care. Once this was over, the car would be dumped, and the false identity he had rented it under would be untraceable. He was no amateur.

He ignored the speed limits, powering the deliberately unremarkable Ford Focus around tight bends and between parked cars, dismissing all rules of right-of-way, bringing angry beeps and shouts from other motorists. It was a risk he had to take, hoping that the lack of police cars he had noted during his short stay would continue for a little while longer.

Heddison had fewer miles to travel but would be carefully obeying all the rules of the road, not taking any chances.

Dennis smiled grimly. He *had* to take those chances.

He pulled on the wheel, swerving, narrowly missing a car edging too far out of its driveway, swearing over his shoulder as he pushed the accelerator to the floor.

Heddison was illegally squatting in an old, abandoned storage shed off the main roads and protected from view by high hedges. Dennis had located it on his first day in the area. After his research into Heddison, his methods, his personal collecting obsession, it had been easy. Once you understood the man, the rest fell into place.

Following the old local signs for Clacton, he sped through Thorrington, alternating brake and accelerator around the narrow, winding lanes, finally turning down toward St Osyth. Almost there.

Had he not scouted the area previously, he would have missed it. Other than a dirt track barely wide enough for one car breaking the otherwise verdant roadside, there was no sign of the building he knew to be in the field behind the hedges, and no sign of Heddison's van.

He swung into the gap, his back wheels spinning on the dirt, unworried about alerting Heddison to his presence. Even allowing for heavy traffic, Heddison would have arrived at least ten minutes ago and would by now be oblivious to almost anything except his victim. The original plan no longer applied. Stealth and subtlety were not an option if he wanted to interrupt Heddison with his Candy Lady.

In a cloud of dust, he skidded the car to a stop near a weathered clapboard building, flayed skin of pale green paint peeling from the wood, lying scab-like on the well-trod ground. Weeds, running wild through neglect, insinuated themselves between the planks and forced them outward, giving the wall a bloated, pregnant look. Window shutters hung from broken hinges, and rusted corrugated iron sheets slipped over the edges of the roof. And yet, it was not possible to see inside the building as all gaps, holes, and windows had been painstakingly covered from the inside. This illegal squatter needed privacy to work.

Hurrying from his car, Dennis found Heddison's silver van parked round the back near the door. He hesitated. The heavy wood of the door was as old as everything else, but the hinges and lock were new and sturdy. He would not be able to break it down. This close, he could hear faint sounds from within, his Candy Lady, Andrea, pleading, begging, her voice growing weaker as he listened. Despite his rising panic, he had no choice. He had to pick the lock.

It was a difficult one to crack, took him almost thirty seconds, but he knew he'd get it. He was good at what he did.

He pushed through the unlocked door, through a small room that may once have been an office, and into the open storage area where Heddison stood in the glow of candlelight and a single 60-watt bulb hanging from a frayed cord in the center of the ceiling. Normally, it was a sight that Dennis would have admired, and even in his current agitated state, he could not completely suppress his aesthetic appreciation of the ambiance Heddison had created. But the reality of how much the delay of the tractor at the harbor had cost him hit him in the stomach like a heavy fist, and he gasped, feeling nauseous, light-headed once more.

The Candy Lady's pink skirt, the one that had first caught his attention, was pinned to the side wall by two six-inch nails. It had been tastefully sliced in a zig-zag pattern, and a strip of flayed skin trailed delicately from the hem. It was a beautiful touch and one he would, at any other time and with any other victim, have appreciated. The purple t-shirt hung next to it, gripped by pale, delicate fingers. Five nails formed a star shape where they had been driven through the back of her hand and into the wall. Blood still dripped from the severed wrist, trailing an abstract pattern of dots and dashes down the wall to the floor. Heddison had already taken his trophy, another for his growing collection, and Dennis's heart seemed to stop for a moment, causing him to clutch at his chest.

The girl herself, Andrea, his Candy Lady, minus a hand and a long strip of skin from her leg, was tied naked and spread-eagled backward over a large wooden barrel. She was alive, despite the loss of blood from her severed hand, but her position, her open-legged nakedness, and the semen spotting her inner thighs were heartbreaking evidence of his failure.

She had seen him, was pleading with her eyes, tearful and dull as she fought to hold onto life. He forced a smile, knowing as he did that this unfamiliar and unwelcome emotion, this *love* that had bludgeoned its way into his heart, his head, was of little use now other than as a source of heavy, deep pain. He could not save his Candy Lady, but he could salvage his original purpose in traveling to Heddison's Stalking Ground. Was that callous? A stubborn voice told him *yes*, but his professionalism and long-time devotion to the collection said *no*, just common sense.

Heddison himself had been slow to sense the other's presence. Indeed, Dennis thought it was probably his Candy Lady and her pleading moan in his direction that first made the killer turn and notice him.

Naked and aroused, with a bloodied hacksaw in one hand and an equally bloodied hammer in the other, Heddison roared in surprise and anger and ran at him.

Dennis, on more familiar ground, was disappointed. He had expected better.

He sidestepped the clumsy swing of the hammer, pulling his favored nine-inch, serrated dagger from its sheath nestling beneath his shirt at the base of his spine, and plunged it deep into Heddison's six-pack. The wet sound of metal sliding into flesh and muscle sent a thrill of excitement through him, and he twisted the blade before withdrawing it with an even louder and more satisfying *slop*. Bits of Heddison fell to the floor in gobbets of blood and gore from the hole the dagger had made. The pattern was random but effective.

With a minimum of movement, Dennis drew the blade across the back of the other man's leg, severing the hamstring. As that leg crumbled beneath the naked man and he began to fall, Dennis stabbed lightly, with small penetration only, into the kidneys. The pain inflicted was excruciating, as evidenced by Heddison's surprisingly high-pitched scream, but the damage not enough to kill.

Dennis nudged the falling man, turning him so he landed on his back, and removed the hammer and hacksaw from him with no resistance. Heddison glared at him through his agony.

Glancing back to his wide-eyed Candy Lady, struggling

to watch the action, he smiled at her once more, but already he could feel the emotion draining, withering, beaten down by the overriding compulsion that had led him to his chosen profession.

He used the hacksaw to remove Heddison's right hand, in a tribute to the killer's own collection, and taking hold of his still erect penis, which was quite impressive in itself, he sawed at the root until it pulled free. For a moment, as the mutilated man screamed and writhed on the floor beneath him, Dennis stopped and admired the spurts and pooling of blood forming a piece of modern art that, he felt, would not be out of place in the Tate Gallery.

Aware that death was fast overtaking the man on the floor, he took his knife once more and gouged out the eyes with a sharp twisting of the blade to ensure nice, round, bloody holes. He used Heddison's own hammer to knock out the teeth and, finally, the hacksaw to separate the head from the body. He liked to use a fellow collector's own tools wherever possible. He considered it only decent and fair.

His Candy Lady, weak from blood loss, stared at him, frightened but relieved it was all over. He smiled and walked to her.

"Hello, Andrea. I'm sorry I wasn't quicker. I tried." To his surprise, there were tears in his eyes, and he wiped them away, staring at his damp hand in wonder. This was all so strange. He leaned closer to the still-bound form of his Candy Lady, whispered, "I love you," and knew it was true. For the first time in his life, he had experienced love, something he had not felt even for his mother back before she abandoned him. It was powerful, almost overwhelming, but ultimately useless and, as thrills go, could not compare to collecting.

He pulled his blade across her exposed throat.

The shock and surprise in her eyes were pleasing, as were the ribbons of blood from the gash in her neck, but it was not true pleasure, just a necessity he found vaguely saddening. She was not the one he had come for.

Kneeling on the floor, holding the severed head of the serial killer firmly between his thighs, he sewed the toothless mouth closed using a surgical needle and thread from the sewing kit he always carried on his belt, small, neat stitches sealing the lips in a karmic smile. Early in his career, he had sewed the eyelids closed, too, but as his collection progressed, he preferred to admire the bloodied eye sockets in their open, sightless gaze.

He lifted the head in admiration. A fine addition.

While it might be true that the serial killers like Heddison who collected trophies of their victims were serious collectors, he was the one and only *supreme* collector.

He collected the collectors.

For the Love of Children

The mewling cry of babies woke Bill Charlotte at 2:00 a.m. For a moment, disoriented and only half-conscious, he wondered why Mary hadn't already gotten out of bed and fed them. Then he remembered that there were no babies and Mary… Mary had died a year ago to the day.

The crying stopped as he sat himself up. It always did. Harsh reality swept away all remnants of dreams and hallucinations, leaving him empty, alone in a five-bedroom family house too big for an 83-year-old widower whose only companions were memories and guilt.

* * *

In the beginning, the only signs of the nightmare to come were lapses in her long-term memory and some confusion over people's names. They laughed it off, putting it down to age, worrying more about Bill's ongoing heart problems than Mary's vagueness. They could cope, had even turned down the offer from their doctor to involve Social Services. They had no children, no brothers or sisters, and throughout their married life had been self-sufficient, independent. Pride and stubbornness refused to let that go.

The only weakness, as Bill saw it, was Mary's occasional slip into broodiness.

"Do you ever regret not having children, Bill?"

It seemed a subject that reared its seditious head every few years or so, and Bill felt compelled to crush it, not giving any quarter, any room for doubt to undermine their years alone together.

"No, never. We agreed, children are a burden. We couldn't afford them, and we never needed them. We made the right choice."

Mary would invariably nod slowly in agreement, and the matter would rest for a while, although the shadow of wistful dreams in her eyes told Bill it would not disappear completely.

The truth was he did have doubts, did wonder if they'd made the right decision all those years ago. Now, as they grew older and their increasing frailty became more inescapable, he sometimes wished he had a son or a daughter to call upon, to ask for occasional help, and, as Mary's dementia took an ever stronger hold, to share his worries with and shore up his resolve. He was not a weak man, but Mary had always been the stronger in the relationship.

As her long-term memory all but dissolved, she would insist they had never been to places he would mention in passing, places they had visited time and again over the years. He would not argue the point.

Their annual Christmas card list became shorter and shorter as she denied ever knowing many of the names on there. Bill would say nothing and cross them off.

She insisted she would continue her habit of a daily walk until she was incapable, and no, he could not go with her. Bill would open the door for her, say goodbye and then sit and worry whether she would remember where she lived.

When she came home from one such walk with the first baby, Bill was horrified, stunned, and unable to do anything other than step aside and let her through the door.

"Look at our daughter, Bill; isn't she lovely? I'm so happy we have a child now, just like we always wanted."

"Mary," he whispered, staring at the bundle in her arms. "What have you done? Where did you…"

"I almost forgot about her," interrupted Mary. "Came out of the shop and had almost forgotten I'd left her outside. I tried to push the pram, but the wheels were jammed or something, so I thought I'd just carry her home." The baby reached up, grabbing Mary's finger in its tiny hand. Mary cooed and smiled.

He should have called the police, Social Services, anyone, but he was scared of what would happen. Scared of them taking Mary away. Scared of Mary's rapidly decaying mental health. He did not know what to do, so he did nothing.

The TV news and daily papers carried the story the next morning. They called it an opportunistic baby snatch from a pram left outside the local greengrocers while the mother was inside. The streets had been quiet. No one had seen anything.

Mary was not capable of caring for the baby, and Bill was too frightened of questions if he bought baby food, so he tried to feed her what little they had in the cupboards. He did not know how to manage.

The baby died two weeks after Mary brought her home.

Bill buried the body in the garden.

* * *

Mary was heartbroken at the loss. She cried. She refused to eat. She blamed him, the world, god. Eventually, she began begging, pleading with Bill that they should have another baby. When he said it was impossible, her pleading turned to anger, to hate, to vitriol.

"You never loved me. If you truly loved me, you'd give me the child I always wanted. I don't want to be with you anymore. I hate you!"

Eventually, as she knew he would, Bill gave in.

It was easier than he expected. Young mothers seemed so careless with their babies that it was not long before he was able to give Mary the second daughter she craved.

He was sick for days afterward, but Mary was content, cooing and smiling but devoid of any basic, practical caring.

The police investigation was detailed and very public but did not include the elderly couple who kept to themselves in their old, detached house.

The baby died just like the first one.

Bill buried it in the garden.

* * *

For a while, Mary seemed calm, content in the blankets, clothes, and soothers she had kept despite Bill's concern that all evidence of the babies should be removed. At times, he doubted she even realized the baby was gone, as she sat holding the blankets, folding, unfolding, and refolding the corners, rocking back and forth, speaking softly to herself.

It seemed her obsession, her delusion, had passed. He was sad at the death of the two babies, did his best not to think about the distress caused to the two mothers, but was relieved that they had gotten away with it.

Then Mary began begging, pleading for another baby, and Bill knew that he had no choice.

* * *

Lying back in the bed on the anniversary of Mary's death, Bill sobbed, sorry for himself, sorry for Mary's death, sorry for the babies buried in the garden. Five in total. Five babies before he had finally snapped and covered her face with the same baby blankets she had collected from each one, covered her mouth and her nose until her weak struggles had stopped and she could no longer beg and plead for more babies.

He had hidden all evidence, of course, before calling the doctor to pronounce Mary dead of natural causes. There was no autopsy, her age and long-term illness were proof enough for a busy, tired doctor.

He still heard her downstairs in the kitchen most mornings, before reality crashed in and destroyed him all over again. He'd been told such things would pass. It had been a year. How long would he have to wait?

And the babies. The crying. He didn't think he'd ever be free of the nightmares that woke him most mornings. How could he forget what he and Mary had done? How could he be clear of the guilt, the horror?

His hand reached out and drew open the bedside cabinet drawer, feeling inside, fingers closing on the soft material of baby blankets, baby clothes. He had not been able to throw them away or destroy them. They were all he had left. As hard as it had been to accept, and as much as he missed Mary, he missed their baby girls, too.

The tiredness of age gradually overcame his thoughts, dampened the turmoil in his brain. He had almost fallen asleep when the mewling sound started again.

The only light came from the digital clock throwing a pale blue wash over his side of the bed, a patch of thin carpet, and the old chair still holding a ball of wool from when Mary used to knit. This time it was no dream. He knew he was awake and refused to believe he was imagining the mournful, pitiful sound.

Despite the fear that tightened in his chest, he had to know the truth. It had to end now. He could no longer live with the fear and guilt.

His feet found the warmth of his slippers on the cold floor, and he shuffled out onto the landing, frightened but stubborn and determined enough to see it through however hard his heart pounded, his pulse raced, and sweat prickled to life on his forehead, dribbling down and tickling the end of his nose.

The babies still cried, and once out of the bedroom, he could tell they were behind the closed door to the extension, somewhere down the corridor near Mary's room.

He hesitated. He had not gone near Mary's room since long before she died. It was *her* room, her place to be alone among her own things. He had always suspected it held collections of cheap pottery and unwearable clothes from her frequent trips to the local charity shops, but he had never questioned or dared to intrude. Even now, he was nervous about entering without being able to ask her first.

The door to the extension corridor swung open easily, and he fumbled for the light switch just inside. The crying was louder, the darkness in the corridor solid, the switch somehow moved from where it should be. He could feel himself beginning to panic, tried to stay calm, kept checking the wall. He found it, flicked the switch, and light flooded the corridor. He was relieved to find it empty, unsure of what he had expected.

Despite the sweat that dripped from the end of his nose, Bill felt cold. The crying had stopped, but he had come too far to turn back now. The answer, he was sure, lay in Mary's room.

Breathing hard and feeling every muscle in his body aching, he entered the room and stopped, surrounded by the clutter of Mary's life, struck by the smell of old things, of undisturbed dust and dirt, and something else he could not place.

The accumulation of junk, of broken toys and children's books and baby clothes, was worse than he had expected.

Then his eyes focused on the walls, and he felt the chill deepen, his stomach turn. Papered with images cut from newspapers, magazines, books, all of babies and small children, there was little of the original wallpaper showing. He had never realized her questions about children hid such an obsession.

In one corner sat a lone trunk, the kind well-off people would take on board cruise liners in the 1920s and 30s. It was noticeable because it was clear of clutter, the only item of furniture not buried beneath piles of baby things. On its top was one item, a large scrapbook. He opened it.

Inside was full of newspaper clippings of baby beauty contests, notices of births, old school pictures, but as he turned further into the book, the clippings became more grim and macabre: baby snatched from pram outside the shop; baby taken while the mother pushed her toddler on the swings in the park; babies taken, kidnapped, stolen. A catalog of their crimes.

He pushed the scrapbook off the trunk, uncaring as it lay half-open, pages buckled, on the floor.

He felt sick and scared but could not stop. He knew he had to look inside the trunk. Inside was the answer to all his questions. He knew this. He was certain.

Pulling open the lid, he staggered quickly backward, gagging at the stench that rose from within, letting it slam closed as he turned, doubled over, and vomited.

He felt light-headed, unsteady, as he straightened up. He had never experienced anything so foul as the smell from the trunk, but he knew he had to try again, and this time he needed to hold out long enough to see what the cause was.

Holding his breath, trying to ignore the nausea, the dizziness, the pain in his chest and arms, he lifted the lid once more and nervously peered inside.

He barely refrained from vomiting again. Inside the trunk, lying as haphazardly as everything else in the room, were the skeletal remains of five babies. The smell came from the rotting flesh that still clung, stubbornly, to some of the bones, flesh that crawled with maggots. The bottom of the trunk was thick with soil from the garden and liquefied remains.

Every time he had buried one of the babies, Mary had gone out and dug it up again, keeping them here in her room, in her trunk, unable to let go. The baby clothes and blankets were just the periphery of her obsession; here was its focus, keeping her daughters alive in her memory, what little remained.

He stepped back, the lid falling against the wall, staying open.

Behind him, he heard a sigh, a contented, blissful sigh he recognized with a deep chill in his stomach and a further tightening of his chest.

Mary!

She stood in the doorway, dressed in the clothes he had buried her in, her face gaunt, cadaverous, gray but smiling.

"I had to come back for my girls, my beautiful babies. We need to be together, always."

And behind him, Bill heard the clattering of bones squelching in the semi-liquid mess at the bottom of the trunk. Mary's five "daughters" clambered from their resting place moments before his heart finally gave out and he fell to the floor, wondering if his bones would form the final piece in Mary's collection.

Castle Ruins

"You've done it now."

David ignored his younger brother and watched as the head of the statue rocked, tipped, and fell. It landed with a *thump* in the long grass, disturbing the thick mist that lay across the ground. The head rolled, just once, before resting on its side, staring at him. Accusing.

"It was an accident," he said, turning to the others. "You saw it was an accident. Right?"

"You were the one swinging that thing around," said Jill, pointing to the rusty sword in David's fist.

"You've *really* done it now."

"Will you shut up?" David spat the words angrily at his brother, Tom, taking his guilt out on the fifteen-year-old.

In the strained silence that followed, he looked at the sword, found earlier in a heap of rubble, as though it were something alien, a thing with a life of its own. He dropped it and stepped back, afraid, just for a moment, that it might fly up and cut off *his* head, too. The thick, oily mist coiled around the sword, caressing it.

"It must have been loose anyhow," said Jill, seeing the blood rising in David's face. "No way that old blade could have cut through stone like that."

David closed his eyes, breathed deeply, counted one... two... three... all the way up to ten just like his counselor told him. Almost unthinking, he snapped the elastic band on his wrist. Another of the counselor's ideas. Jill was right. He had to believe that. The rusty, old sword couldn't have cut through the stone.

"I was only winding you up," said Tom, having learned painfully over the years when it was wise to step back and calm down his brother. "Like Jill said, the thing must have been loose. You hardly touched it, and it just fell off."

David nodded, letting the rage that had momentarily threatened to rise dissipate in the thickening mist. They were right. He shouldn't blame himself for an accident. He shouldn't blame them either.

He turned his back on the headless statue, on the accusing face in the grass, and for the first time saw the castle rearing up out of the mist not more than fifty feet away.

"I never knew there was a castle up here," he said, taking a step toward it, the statue already forgotten.

"I thought it was just these old gardens and ruins," said Jill, hurrying to his side. "That's what my dad said anyway."

"Well, your dad was wrong," said Tom. "Unless we're all seeing things, like David."

Jill threw him a warning look, but if David even heard the comment, he didn't react. He was too busy walking toward the castle, looking up at it in wonder.

"We've got to go in," said David. "Get a closer look."

"Are we allowed to?" said Tom.

"Are you scared you'll be told off?" David glanced back at his brother. "Or just frightened of the big, bad castle?"

Tom looked down at the mist-covered ground, annoyed with himself. "I'm not scared."

"Of course you are," said David, sneering. "You're scared of just about everything."

"David," said Jill, placing a hand on his arm. "Enough. Leave him alone."

For a moment, David hesitated, as though he wanted to say something more, but then he turned and walked away. Jill hurried to catch him up, waving at Tom to follow.

"It's fantastic," said David, smiling. Any tension was forgotten as he studied the ancient stonework in front of him.

"You know a bit about castles," said Jill as she reached him. "Why's that window up there so small?"

David followed Jill's pointing finger to the narrow slit high up on the wall.

"That's an arrow-loop," he said. "The castle archers would fire through that at the enemy out here. You'll see them on the other walls as well."

David led the way round to the left. Before she followed, Jill smiled at Tom, just reaching her, and he nodded in return. They both had ways to distract and calm David when needed.

Less than two minutes later, they found the great arched gateway. Tom thought the portcullis hung a little precariously, one-third of the way down.

"What now?" said Tom. "I don't see any signs with opening times. Maybe it's not open to the public?"

"You can do what you like," said David. "I'm going in."

Without another word or any sign of hesitation, David ducked under the portcullis and strode through, disappearing into the deep shadows thrown by the gateway.

Jill watched him go, unsure whether to follow. Tom was looking at the sky. Behind the rising mist, it was growing dark. He checked his watch.

"What time did we come out?" he said.

"I don't know," said Jill. "About two. Why?"

"It's getting dark, and my watch says it's almost nine-thirty. Surely we've not been out that long?"

Jill pulled her phone from her back pocket. "21:28," she said. "We must have been longer than we thought getting up here."

She didn't believe it herself but had no wish to unsettle Tom further. He already looked ready to run. "Come on," she said. "Let's follow David before we lose him altogether."

They found David just inside the main entrance, standing at the edge of the courtyard. In the gathering gloom, it was difficult to make out much detail, but there were several handcarts scattered around, a hay bale, and straight ahead of them, a well. David, without even acknowledging that the others had joined him, headed straight for the well.

He turned back as he reached it and called, "Come here. Take a look at this."

"What about it?" asked Tom as he and Jill hurried across

the open courtyard to stand by the well.

"Don't you see?" asked David. The other two shook their heads. "There's no bars, no safety barriers, nothing covering the well at all. When have you ever seen a well that's escaped Health and Safety?"

Jill crossed her arms, pressing them in tight against her chest. She shivered.

"I don't like it," she said almost in a whisper. "There's something not right about this place."

The mist from outside seemed to curl a little higher, climbing up the walls. It twisted around the base of the well, stray fingers crawling over the edge, disappearing down into complete darkness.

Tom looked around nervously, unsettled by how quickly the night had closed in. He stared upward at the angular shadows thrown by the castle towers, the moon all but hidden behind them, and shuddered.

"I still don't think we should be here."

"Come on," said David, ignoring the doubts of the others. "Let's go inside the Keep."

"David," said Jill, the slight shake in her voice coming from more than just the cool night air. "I'm not sure. I think we should stay outside."

"Or even better, leave," said Tom. "Please, David, I don't like it here."

David laughed. "You're just scared, both of you."

"Yes," said Jill. "Yes, I'm afraid; I'll admit it."

"But what are you afraid of?" said David. "It's an old castle. Even better, an old castle that hasn't been spoiled by stupid regulations."

"I'm scared," said Tom, drawing closer to Jill.

"You're always scared," sneered David.

"Leave him alone." Jill put an arm around Tom's shoulders, feeling suddenly protective. She and David might have gone to school together, but sometimes she felt she had more in common with Tom. Particularly when it came to dealing with David.

"Why are there no signs?" said Tom. "There's always signs telling you where to go, what different things are, even pointing to the gift shop. I've never been in a place with no signs before."

"He's right," said Jill. "And my dad said it was only a ruin up here, and he should know."

"He's a postman, not a historian," said David, contempt dripping from his voice with almost visible venom.

Jill shuddered. David's bad side was beginning to show.

"He knows the area, David. This should be a ruin!"

David's laugh echoed from the stone walls, seemed to rise out of the well before them, disturbing the mist like an oil slick spreading across the waves.

"Does it look like a ruin to you? Your dad's full of crap!" David spun on his heel and strode toward the Keep. "Do whatever you want. I'm going in."

The Keep was all but pitch black inside, a little moonlight sneaking in through gaps in the old stonework. David didn't care. He felt he could guess the layout pretty well. He'd always had an interest in castles. All the more surprising that he had never known about this one right on his doorstep.

Straight ahead of him would be the Main Hall. To the right the Armory, probably the Knights' Quarters, too. To the left would be the Chapel. There'd be other rooms, too, away from the Main Hall, down narrow stone corridors. A Kitchen; food storage; the servants' quarters. In the dark, he could almost imagine how it must have been, back when it was not just some historical pile of stones, but a home, a fortress. He could almost hear the sounds of footsteps, of voices, the bustling of servants, and the boisterous laughter of those they served.

Only he wasn't imagining it.

He really *was* hearing the sounds of people around him, of movement and laughter. He could smell the ale, the meat roasting. He could smell the people, earthy, sweaty.

For the first time, David was scared.

* * *

"What was that?" said Tom, quickly turning to look back toward the main entrance into the courtyard.

"I didn't hear anything," said Jill. "What…?"

She could hear it now. Distant, echoing hoofbeats, quickly coming closer, the echo tightening until it became no more than the stone walls about them throwing the sound back and forth. Horses. She could smell the sweat of a hard ride on them, hear the snorting and neighing close by. But she could see nothing but the courtyard walls, the silhouette of towers reaching into the sky, the mist angry and swirling as though things moved through it, things she could not see.

But she could see Tom, terrified, frozen in fear.

Something brushed past her. She staggered but did not fall. Another caught her shoulder, yet another her side. She stepped back to the well, clinging onto the low wall, hoping to stay out of the way of…she didn't know what!

Tom, seeing Jill move to the well and having felt something pass nearby himself, hurried to join her. They clutched hands together, faces pale, eyes wide with fear.

"What's going on?" said Tom, his voice shaking. "What's happening?"

The mist in the courtyard rose higher still, its movement erratic, constant, disturbed!

* * *

Was this one of his hallucinations?

It was a question David had to ask himself, even though it was like nothing he had ever experienced before.

He tried closing his eyes, counting to ten, distraction by snapping the elastic band on his wrist, but the sounds and the smells remained. He had seen things before, but he had never heard and smelled them. This was different, unique.

Perhaps, just perhaps, it wasn't a hallucination after all. Maybe it was real!

Was that really better?

The noise increased, closed in. It felt like a coffin being built around him, the lid hammered into place by the sudden hammering of a meat cleaver into a wooden table. It pressed against him, tighter and tighter, until he could barely breathe.

"Stop it!" he shouted, pushing back against the sound, a

scream more than a shout. "Shut up! Shut up!"

The conversation faltered around him, the pressure of sound easing off. Feet shuffled to a stop.

He opened his eyes and, for the first time, could see vague shadows of people, trailing mist with each movement as though they were made of smoke. They were all around him, standing, sitting, eating, drinking. He saw a large, barrel-chested figure of darkness rise to stand above those seated about it, and the roar of a voice silenced those few still talking.

"Who commanded we stop?"

David ran for the Main Hall exit. It was all he could think to do, driven by fear.

He never imagined that they would be able to see him any better than he could see them, until he heard the voice roar, "Stop him! Get the boy!"

* * *

Shadowy shapes of horses and riders began to coalesce out of the swirling mist as Jill and Tom stood hand in hand by the well. Dark shapes drew near to them, away again, as though curious but unsure.

A deep voice spoke near Jill's ear, making her shudder.

"What have we here? A damsel fit for my chamber, perhaps?"

Jill tried to pull away, to reach for Tom, as mist-trailed fingers grasped her arm and tugged.

Tom, seeing that Jill was in danger, took her other arm and pulled her toward him.

Jill, powerless in the tug-of-war, screamed.

"Let her go!" shouted Tom. "Let her go, or I'll—"

"Peasant."

The single word, spoken so close to Tom that he felt a breath of stale air strike his cheek, startled him, and he loosened his grip on Jill's arm. He turned his head and was faced with the deep, impenetrable blackness of a creature that, even without eyes, seemed to be peering at him with contempt. Mist curled off the top like stray wisps of hair.

"Begone!"

The blackness lurched forward, pushing Tom in the chest, hard, the shadowy hands seeming to sink beneath his skin.

Tom staggered, felt the wall of the well against the back of his legs, and began to lose his balance.

Jill watched, horrified, still struggling against the grip on her arm, as Tom fell backward. She saw him look toward her, his mouth open, his eyes wide with fear, and then he toppled into the black hole of the well.

She heard him cry out as he fell, his voice echoing, quickly disappearing in the distance. A dull splash, an even duller *thud*.

Jill screamed louder than she had ever screamed before.

* * *

David heard the scream, pushed himself harder. He was out of the Main Hall, running down the short corridor toward the courtyard. Behind him, shadows filled the spaces, tumbling over each other to be the first to reach him.

He burst into the open air of the courtyard and skidded to a halt, horrified by the swirling mass of human and animal shapes milling around in front of him. They were everywhere!

He could see no sign of Tom.

Another scream. He turned and saw Jill struggling with two, maybe three, vaguely human forms of darkness. The mist around them danced with fury at the angry movements.

She saw him. "David! Help!"

He glanced behind, back toward the Keep. His pursuers erupted from the entrance, agitated, searching. He looked over to Jill, still struggling, still staring at him in hope and desperation. He wondered again where Tom was.

He decided to save himself.

Ignoring the screams of disbelief and anger from Jill, he ran for the castle gateway. He dodged the black shapes of horses, ducked under the occasional grasping, shadowy arm, aware that the creatures from the Main Hall had spotted him and were chasing.

He ran harder and faster than he had ever run before, shutting out the smells around him, the impossibility of the shapes in the darkness, the desperation and hatred in Jill's slowly dying screams. Head down, he made it through, remembering at the last minute to duck beneath the hanging portcullis. It scraped the top of his head.

He was out, stumbling, falling into the mist, onto the soft grass of the hillside.

Everything was quiet. The silence was thick in his head after the noise of the castle. There was nothing but the occasional car horn down in the town, a bat darting by overhead.

Fearfully, he looked back toward the castle gateway. Nothing. No dark shapes pushing out, looking for him. No horses. No angry pursuers.

No Jill or Tom.

Stunned, feeling oddly detached, numb even, he climbed to his feet and made his way back, following the castle wall once again.

He kept glancing behind, afraid he might, at any moment, see dark figures looming up. He stopped every few steps and listened, but there was nothing out of the ordinary to be heard.

He reached the open ground, began to quicken his step to get away from the castle.

Looking back, he saw the stone wall rising out of the mist. He thought he saw movement behind the narrow slit high up.

The arrow flew silent and straight, a jet-trail of mist swirling in its wake. It penetrated the calf muscle of David's left leg, punching out the other side, cracking the shinbone.

He cried out in sudden agony, fell, staring in disbelief at the black arrow that dissipated into tendrils of mist, curling away, leaving only the bloody hole in his leg.

The mist in front of him stirred, agitated as something rose out of it—an old, rusty sword. The same sword David had found earlier. The same sword he had swung and broken the statue with.

The sword, not held by any visible hand, arced back. David looked at it, scared but curious. How was it floating?

It sliced downward, oily trails of mist spiraling around it.

* * *

The ruins of Gaskell Castle stood, as they had for many years, on the breast of the hill above the town of Gaskell. The outer wall was nothing but a broken line of stones in the ground, the inner courtyard overgrown and, except for two picnic benches, empty. A sealed metal door covered the hole where the well had once been. Nothing remained of the Keep other than some small collections of rubble where walls had once stood. It was no longer possible to discern where the Main Hall had been.

Out in the gardens of Gaskell Castle stood the statue of a man holding a sword aloft. The stone head lay in the long grass some feet from the base, no longer needed. In its place on the stone neck was the open-eyed, bloodied head of a young man.

David stared at the castle ruins. He could do nothing else.

Emily in the Wall

Anna Kolton had been seeing people in the walls since the accident.

Her doctors said it was Post Traumatic Stress Disorder. A malfunctioning of her brain due to shock and stress. Watching a number 75 bus bounce over the curb and barrel toward you at forty miles an hour will do that to you, apparently. She couldn't remember the impact, just the big box of metal getting closer, the look of horror on the face of the driver, still clear to her after all these years, and her complete inability to move. Since then, she'd seen the people in the walls.

"Can they see you as well, Anna?"

That was Kenneth Gildersleeve, Ph.D., her latest therapist—and the most patronizing, *smarmy* person she had ever met.

"Well, none of them have waved and said hello yet, if that's what you mean."

It was difficult not to be sarcastic with *Ken*, as he insisted she call him.

"Now, Anna. You know what I mean."

She sighed. "No. As far as I can tell, they don't see me."

"And do you see them all the time?" He glanced over toward the far wall. "For instance, do you see them now? In that wall over there?"

"No, I don't see them all the time," said Anna, with more patience than she would have given herself credit for. "Just sometimes. And before you ask, I have no idea what might trigger it."

"Do they make any sounds at all, Anna?"

"No. It's like watching a silent movie. Haven't we been through all this before?"

Ken smiled his supercilious smile. Anna wanted to punch him.

"I know, Anna. But you must understand how important it is that I get a sense of how consistent these visions are."

"They're not visions! There are people living out their lives in the walls!"

"Of course, there are, Anna. I understand that this is real to you, but—"

And then Anna *did* punch him.

* * *

It wasn't every day that people saw a young woman in a wheelchair being escorted out of the clinic by two burly security men. That was why so many stopped and stared.

"He deserved it," shouted Anna as they wheeled her out of the automatic doors. "The smug prick!"

The security guards left her outside, but not before one of them had given her a smile and a wink that said he agreed with her. That cheered her up a little.

Everything she had told him was true. She had no idea why she sometimes saw the people and other times not. And there was no sound. She wished there was. Most of all, she wished they could see her. Then, perhaps, she could find some way to communicate.

* * *

The following morning, steering her motorized chair toward the nearby local shops, she passed the brick wall that bordered the new housing estate. Sometimes she saw *visitors* there, but mostly it was just brick. Today, there were people walking along a street not dissimilar to her own, and she did not pay them much attention. Until she saw the girl.

She looked younger than Anna, maybe in her mid to late teens, and was also in a wheelchair. Not a motorized one, but a simpler, push-along one. It was the first time Anna had seen someone in a wheelchair among the *visitors*. She found it both reassuring, because there were people like her wherever the *visitors* lived, and unnerving because it was a little like looking into a fairground mirror that not only distorted your image, but reality, too.

Anna stopped and watched for a little while as an older woman pushed the girl along. The girl looked unhappy, and Anna experienced a deep feeling of empathy. She knew that look. She saw it in the mirror every day.

Feeling her own loneliness, her own depression, weighing heavily, she decided to move on. There was nothing she could do to help the girl. She could barely help herself most days.

And then the girl turned, looked right at her, and waved.

* * *

"Fuck me!" The words exploded from Anna before she had chance to think. She quickly apologized to the elderly couple walking by and hoped she wasn't blushing too much.

The girl can see me. Can anyone else?

The woman pushing the girl continued walking, uninterested in the girl's waving, and she was obviously unaware of Anna. Cautiously, Anna raised her arm and waved back. Knowing she must look a complete fool waving to a brick wall, she kept the movement short.

The excited, fast waving from the girl proved to Anna, beyond a doubt, that the girl could see her.

Anna watched until the girl was wheeled out of sight, off the edge of the wall, and then went home. Her mind was too full of questions, of confusing thoughts, to go shopping. She needed to think.

* * *

The brick wall did not offer up the *visitors* every day, nor was the girl always there when it did. But she did return on a reasonably regular basis and, over the following week or two, Anna and the girl exchanged waves, and even an occasional mouthing of words. Anna thought the girl said her name was Emily, but she couldn't be sure. Nevertheless, it was a name, and, right or wrong, the girl in the wheelchair, in the wall, was Emily.

The moments of communication were short. The woman pushing Emily's wheelchair never stopped, never even slowed, just kept on pushing. What she thought of Emily's strange behavior, if she even noticed it, Anna had no idea. The woman had a sad, dazed look on her face. She probably didn't take much notice of anything.

Back in her apartment, Anna had already Googled *Emily in a wheelchair* and similar search phrases, spending hours looking at pictures and scouring social media pages. No one even remotely resembled Emily in the wall. It did not really surprise her. She felt in her gut that the world in the wall was somewhere *else*. She did not know where, but it was not *here*.

* * *

Over the next two months, Anna gradually became aware that Emily's hurt went much deeper than her own. There was something always there, even when the girl was smiling and waving. A bitter backdrop of despair. More than ever, Anna wished she could *speak* to Emily. Ask her where that hurt came from.

The answer eventually came in a way that Anna would never have wanted.

It started with Emily appearing, not in the brick wall of the housing estate, but in Anna's own bedroom wall. And she wasn't being wheeled along a street; she was being wheeled into a bedroom.

The room was dark, with heavy curtains pulled over a small window. Bright sunlight flared through a small gap where the curtains had not been properly drawn, and Anna wondered why the curtains were drawn at all if it was still daylight outside. The walls of the room were bare, no posters or pictures. Just paint, flaking off in places. What Anna could see of the bed seemed okay, but somehow that just emphasized how depressing the rest of the room was.

Emily did not look toward Anna this time. There was no waving. Instead, she sat, slumped, in the wheelchair, dark hair hanging over her face. At first, Anna wondered if she was asleep, but then Emily's head turned, and she looked up as the woman pushing her said something.

The man entered the room behind the woman. He was tall, and so thin the bones showed through his sleeveless t-shirt. An unshaven chin surrounded the cruel slit of a mouth, and the sharp nose and narrow eyes only emphasized the stick insect-like impression Anna had of him. She took an instant dislike to him.

The man and woman did not speak to each other, and it seemed to Anna as though they did not need to. This was a routine done often. The woman turned and left, leaving Emily in her wheelchair by the bed. The man walked to the wheelchair and lifted Emily out of it, holding her in his stick-thin arms. Anna could see Emily's face, and she went cold. Emily's expression was blank, detached. Dissociated. An icy finger ran down Anna's spine. Although Emily was clearly alive, she looked dead.

The man put Emily on the bed and, with slow, calm movements, pushed the wheelchair out of the way. He stood with his back to Anna, blocking much of her view, but she could tell he was removing Emily's clothing.

He could be her father, or a nurse, or her caregiver, Anna told herself, desperately wanting to believe it. *Maybe this is normal?*

She had to accept the horrifying truth as the man began to remove his own clothes.

For the first time, Emily turned her head and looked at Anna. She still had that blank expression on her face, but she was crying, a tear rolling down her cheek to stain the bedsheet.

Wild with rage, Anna drove her wheelchair into the skirting board. She screamed. She hammered on the wall. "Leave her alone, you bastard. You fucker! Leave her alone!"

She kept hitting the wall until her fists bled. Screamed until her voice was hoarse. Sobbed, feeling helpless, *useless*!

Somehow it would be different if she wasn't stuck in her wheelchair. In some way, she would have been able to help Emily if her legs worked.

It made no sense, but she convinced herself. It was her fault for being disabled, for being a cripple. She detested the word, but she used it now. *Cripple.* That's what she was. A cripple, unable to save a young girl from being attacked. Unable to help her one friend.

With her hands bruised and bleeding, the pain just beginning to register, and an intense feeling of guilt that she was relieved she could not hear what was happening in the wall, she finally turned her face away. Unable to watch any more.

She sobbed her anger and frustration. Concerned neighbors were banging on her door, calling out to her, frightened by the screams and shouts they had heard. She did not answer them. She could not leave the bedroom. It felt too much like she was abandoning Emily, and that would be even worse than her inability to physically help her.

She knew she would have to look again. It was not right to just turn away from the abuse her friend was suffering. It was not something that could be just ignored. She forced herself to turn and look.

Emily still lay on the bed, no longer looking at Anna, but staring toward the ceiling. Tears still trickled down her cheek.

Anna stared with hatred at the naked back of the man. She wished so much she could reach through the wall and tear his spine from his body. It would not be difficult. It stood out in clear relief through the hair on his back. She was still imagining the satisfaction she would feel when a cold block of fear quenched the fire of her hatred.

The man in the wall looked back over his shoulder, directly at Anna, and smiled.

* * *

Anna lay in her bed and tried to sleep. For the first time since she'd started seeing the *visitors*, she was afraid to look at the walls. What if she saw more evidence of the abuse suffered by Emily? Abuse Anna was powerless to prevent. Or perhaps the man would know some way to reach out through the wall and enter Anna's world? The guilt she felt at being unable to help Emily was equal to the guilt she felt at worrying about her own safety. And in both cases, she was letting Emily down.

That had to stop.

It was not often that Anna admitted it, but she needed another viewpoint, someone to bounce ideas off. But who could she explain all this to? She had no friends or family. After the accident, it had been the therapy and her own bloody mindedness that got her through.

Therapy.

Perhaps she could talk it out with someone who was paid to listen?

It would mean swallowing some of her stubborn pride. But, given that she could not afford to go private, there was only one person who might be willing to see her without the need to go on a waiting list.

* * *

"Thank you for seeing me," said Anna, putting on her best smile and then adding, for good measure, "Ken."

"I almost didn't," said Kenneth Gildersleeve, lifting fingers to his left eye, remembering.

"I am so sorry about that," said Anna. "I don't—"

"Let's just forget about it, shall we?" Kenneth turned to the computer screen, briefly checking through Anna's records. "It doesn't look like you've seen anyone else since our last session. You really should have seen someone."

"I'd gone off the idea of therapy." Anna watched Kenneth Gildersleeve as he scrolled through the entries on the screen. With the tension between them, he had lost much of the *smarminess* of their earlier encounters. He seemed more genuine, somehow. She found she preferred it.

"So, what made you change your mind? And why me?" Kenneth turned in his seat and faced Anna. There was no smile on his face.

"I really feel I need to talk to someone, and despite our last session, I thought we were, sort of, getting along?"

Kenneth sighed. "Not to mention avoiding the waiting list to see a new therapist."

Anna smiled a little guiltily at being found out so easily.

"So," said Kenneth. "What was it you needed to talk about so desperately?"

* * *

"So you see," said Anna, having laid out the background as best she could and, surprisingly, with no interruptions from *Ken*. "The situation, as I see it, is this."

She took a deep breath before continuing. So far, it had gone better than expected. She just hoped the next part, the most crucial part, and her whole reason for returning to Kenneth Gildersleeve's therapy sessions, went as well. If this didn't help, she was out of ideas.

"I can see the people in the walls. Emily and, by the looks of things, her abuser can see me. Everyone else seems completely oblivious to it all. So, I was thinking there must be some kind of connection between the three of us, right? Something that makes us different from the rest."

Kenneth said nothing but nodded in apparent agreement. He had not once lost his concentration during Anna's long explanation. Despite her antagonism toward him, she was impressed and grateful.

"Both I and Emily are in wheelchairs, obviously," she continued, clasping and unclasping her hands nervously. "I ended up in one because of an accident, but I have no idea how Emily did. Was she like that from birth? Or did she have an accident, too? As for the man? Other than him being a sick fuck, I have no idea."

She stopped and surprised herself by blushing.

"Sorry about the language," she said.

Kenneth waved a hand dismissively. "No problem. I'd probably say the same myself."

"But I can't get any further. And I've still no idea how to help Emily. I know you think I'm imagining all of it, but I have to do something to help."

"Okay," said Kenneth, steepling his fingers, the tips just touching his bottom lip. "Let's get one thing straight. I don't think you're imagining this. I'm not saying it's real, but it's not just your imagination."

He leaned back in his chair, closing his eyes, thinking.

Anna said nothing. Outside the surgery window, the sky had grown overcast. People were beginning to hurry past, pulling on their coats. She guessed it had gotten colder. It was almost certainly going to rain. And she had forgotten her umbrella.

Turning her attention back inside, she saw Ken glance at the clock on the wall. She was aware that they were running over, that she should have left almost twenty minutes ago.

"Will you be in this evening?" he said, catching her off guard. She tried not to look too surprised.

"Why?"

"I have other patients to see, but I think it's important we continue this." He hesitated. "Would you mind if I paid you a visit at home this evening? Say, about seven?"

"No, that's fine," said Anna, wondering why she felt nervous. It wasn't like it was a *date*.

"It'll be off the record. Also, it gives me some time to think about this more. See if I can come up with anything that might help."

"That's great," said Anna, surprised to realize she meant it. "I appreciate your help. You know, you're almost beginning to talk about my world in the wall as though you believe it's real."

Kenneth Gildersleeve smiled. "I suppose I am."

* * *

Anna was surprisingly anxious waiting for Ken to arrive. She told herself it was because they would be discussing Emily and the bastard who was abusing her, but a part of her kept thinking that, bereft of the *smarminess*, Ken Gildersleeve was actually quite handsome.

She felt guilty for thinking that way. This was about Emily and how to help *her*. Not about a potential boyfriend. This evening was absolutely, positively, and in no way a date!

At seven, she waited for the doorbell to ring.

At one minute past seven, she was convinced he had changed his mind and was not coming.

At three minutes past seven, the doorbell rang, and she almost tipped herself out of the wheelchair in her shock.

She let Kenneth in, slightly disappointed he had not brought flowers, or wine, or chocolates, or anything really, other than a pre-packed sandwich, obviously for his own consumption. Then she felt guilty and stupid. This was *not* a date, and it was apparent by his clothes that he had come straight from the surgery.

He raised the sandwich, still unopened, and smiled apologetically. "I didn't want you to have to make me anything, so I grabbed this from the garage on the way."

"That's fine," she said, adequately hiding both her disappointment and her disgust with herself. "I don't cook anyway. Microwave and takeaways for me, I'm afraid."

She led him through to the couch and waited while he made himself comfortable.

"I can do a cup of tea or coffee, however. Would you like one?"

"Tea would be nice, thank you."

Once they were both settled with tea, she said, "Did you manage to come up with anything?"

The directness of the question helped settle her nerves.

Concentrate on the real reason he's here.

"Possibly," said Kenneth, sipping the tea. "This might sound more than a little *Doctor Who*, but I think you're observing a *parallel* universe."

"Parallel universe?" Anna shook her head, a little confused. "I've heard the words, but I've never had to try and understand them before. Does this mean you actually believe me? That you don't think it's all just in my head?"

"Yes, I believe you. Not quite sure why, but I do." Kenneth's mouth stretched into a genuine smile. Anna found she liked it.

"So, explain this parallel universe thing," she said.

"Avoiding topics like the *many worlds interpretation* of quantum mechanics, which nobody truly understands anyway, it's basically the idea that our universe is not alone. There are lots of other universes just like ours running parallel."

"But we don't normally see them?"

"Exactly. There are varying theories, from there being no true connection at all to the whole *multiverse* being in contact on a quantum level all the time. But in all of them, the parallel universe is not normally visible."

"Except this one is, to me."

"Yes."

"But why just one? And why this particular one?"

"I can only guess that it's to do with some connection to Emily," said Kenneth. "That's all presuming I'm right in the first place. About the parallel universe thing, I mean."

"It's weird," said Anna. "But it feels right. The real problem is that it doesn't make it any easier for me to help Emily. I have to save her from that monster."

Kenneth stood and began pacing, back and forth. "There

has to be some way to weaken the barrier between the universes," he said. "Some ritual even. This can't be the first time it's happened."

"Ritual? Are we talking science or magic here?" Anna tried to laugh, but she could not force it.

Kenneth stopped pacing.

"Whatever it takes."

* * *

Anna was sitting up in bed, reading, when she caught the movement on her bedroom wall from the corner of her eye.

She almost didn't look, didn't *want* to look, but she had to know.

It was Emily's bedroom again, as sparse and grim as before. Anna's heart rate quickened, breath shortened, as she watched Emily wheeled in, the man lifting her onto the bed. Just as before, and every bit as horrifying and sickening. Emily turned her head and looked at Anna, despair and pleading in her eyes. This time the man looked back over his shoulder before he took off Emily's clothes. His grin, revealing uneven, yellowed teeth, was a clear message to Anna. It said he knew she was watching and he didn't care because he knew she was powerless to stop him.

With rage barely held in check, Anna mouthed the words very carefully, staring back at the man. *I will kill you.*

The man laughed, and Anna didn't need to hear it to know it would be a confident, vicious laugh. He knew she could not reach him. But she would find a way—with or without Kenneth Gildersleeve's help. She had to.

* * *

"He's enjoying it," said Anna, as she and Kenneth Gildersleeve headed toward the shops. She had called him first thing in the morning, saying she wanted to talk. Not about anything in particular, just talk, and to get out of the apartment. "He knows I can't ignore what's happening, but he's also confident I can't stop him. We have to find a way."

"Unfortunately, ideas on how to intrude on parallel universes are few on the ground, if you ignore all the computer games and fiction around the subject," said Kenneth, his pace slowing as he spoke. Anna slowed to keep alongside him. "However, I did find a couple of experiences similar to yours."

Anna was surprised and guardedly hopeful. "Tell me more."

"In Siberia, back in 1908, a man named Marat Ignatyev was hurt in the Tunguska explosion. You know, the asteroid one?"

Anna nodded. "I've heard of it."

"Well, after receiving this injury, he claimed things were moving around in his walls. He called them ghosts and thought his home was haunted, but maybe he was seeing into another universe, just like you."

"Did he manage to do anything about these ghosts?"

"Afraid not," said Kenneth, sighing. "It would seem it got so bad, he eventually just moved home, and the old place was destroyed."

"Well, I'm not moving home because of this bastard, so that doesn't help," said Anna.

"There were a couple of others, but they didn't solve anything either," said Kenneth. "One was committed to an asylum, the other moved home, like Marat. However..." He smiled. "...What *is* of interest is that, in all three cases, their experiences began after some kind of major trauma. In modern terms, all of them probably suffered from PTSD."

"Just like me," said Anna thoughtfully. "Well done."

Kenneth Gildersleeve looked embarrassed, and Anna thought she had never seen him look so *cute* before.

They walked past the brick wall by the new estate, and Anna glanced toward it. But today, it was just brick. She felt relieved, and then guilty for feeling that way.

"Based on the little we now know," said Kenneth, continuing, not understanding the significance of that particular wall, "you almost certainly became sensitive to the other universe after your accident."

Anna nodded. "And I guess we're presuming a similar thing with Emily?"

"Yes. It's the best we've got."

"That leaves us with the asshole."

Kenneth smiled. "Indeed, it does. Now, it's possible this *asshole* also had some kind of accident, although there's nothing evident to back that up."

"I don't think he had an accident," said Anna. "I think he's just naturally weird. Maybe he's seen our world all his life? For all we know, that could be what's driven him to be the crazy fuck he is now!"

Anna strove to keep her voice down when everything about the situation made her want to shout it out loud.

"None of which helps us find a way to stop him," said Kenneth.

"No," agreed Anna. "But it's more than we had before. Can you give me those names you found? The ones who had similar experiences? I wouldn't mind doing a bit of research myself."

* * *

It seemed *Ken* was right about Marat Ignatyev. There was no extra information on him after he moved house. No one else would live in the *haunted house*, so it had been torn down. There was no record of whether or not Mr. Ignatyev continued to see his *ghosts* after he moved.

One of the other two names, Juno Sumual, was a mixed Irish-Indonesian woman who, in 1883, started seeing people in the walls after her hometown of Merak, on the north-western tip of Java, was destroyed by tsunamis following the eruption of Krakatoa. She was one of the few survivors. Like Marat Ignatyev, she eventually moved house, and there was no reliable record of her after that.

The final case had more potential.

Vito Golini had been a passenger on the Milan–Rome Express when it derailed after hitting a truck on the line in Codogno, Italy, 1957. After several weeks of hospitalization, he had returned home, only to go to the police soon afterward claiming there were people in the walls of his house.

No one believed him. Thankfully, the old police and court records had been transcribed onto the internet, and with help from online translation, Anna was able to read them.

Golini had been persistent, becoming a known irritant to the police. Six months after he filed his first complaint, he started to bring items in to the police, claiming they were from the world within his walls and that they proved he was telling the truth. Unfortunately, they were simple household items such as knives, spoons, and so on, and looked perfectly ordinary. Again, no one believed him. But of most interest to Anna was the part where he explained to the police how he had gotten the objects.

Golini was an early follower of the Eastern yogi Paramahansa Yogananda. He claimed that, by using meditation techniques, he had been able to direct all his strength, all his internal energy, into one hand. Moving slowly, he had then been able to push that hand through the wall in his house and into the other world. It was agony, he said, and not something he could bear to do often.

Vito Golini had eventually been sent to a mental asylum, as much to remove him as a time-waster as anything else. He died in the asylum two years later, insisting that the people in the walls had followed him there. Recorded cause of death was a heart attack.

Anna felt drained after reading Golini's story. Although, in theory, she lived in more *enlightened* times, she wondered how the police would have welcomed her if she had done the same as Vito and gone to *them* with her story rather than a therapist. Would she have ended up being sectioned? It was a scary thought and one she tried to push to the background. Instead, she concentrated on the method he claimed he used to bring objects back from the other world.

Golini had only pushed his *hand* through, which did not seem of any immediate help to Anna. But it gave her some hope in that *something* had been able to pass through to the other side.

Now she needed to try it for herself.

* * *

With Kenneth standing just behind her in case things went badly wrong, Anna tried to push her hand through the wall.

She approached it slowly, pressing her fingers against the plaster, gently pushing, slowly, so slowly…

Nothing happened.

She tried again, even slower.

Nothing.

Again and again and again, until, in sheer frustration, she backed her wheelchair away from the wall and left the bedroom.

Kenneth caught up with her on the ramp up to the kitchen.

"I need a coffee," she said angrily.

"We never thought it would be easy," he said, using his calm therapist voice. A mistake that almost cost him dearly.

Anna turned the wheelchair sharply toward him, catching his knee with the frame.

"Don't talk to me like one of your patients, Ken," she snapped. "I thought we were friends now, not doctor and *nut-*

case!"

"We are friends, Anna," said Kenneth, rubbing his knee to ease the pain. "I'm sorry if you thought I was treating it differently. Maybe sometimes I can't help it?"

"Maybe," said Anna, slowly calming down. "But don't do it again."

"All I was trying to say was that we shouldn't get too frustrated just because it didn't work the first time." He followed Anna into the kitchen area and took the kettle off her, filling it at the tap. "Let's go back over Vito's claims word by word and see if we're missing anything."

Over coffee and tea, they studied the translated text again.

After several readings, both in silence and aloud, Kenneth found the detail he was looking for.

"Paramahansa Yogananda introduced the West to Kriya yoga in the early part of the twentieth century," he said. "It's certainly possible that Vito was a student."

"And you know this how?"

Kenneth smiled apologetically. "One of my tutors at university was heavily into it. I picked up some of the history from him."

"Yes, well," said Anna. "I'm doing my best, but I'm not some kung fu master who can channel their *chi*, or whatever, to different parts of the body at will."

"Yoga, not kung fu. And I don't think Vito was any *master* either. But the meditation techniques he learned almost certainly helped. You ever done any yoga or meditation?"

"Years ago," said Anna. "My first therapist after the accident was big on the importance of meditation, so I tried it for a while."

"Do any good?"

Anna shook her head. "I'm too easily distracted."

"Well, I can teach you a few easy techniques to try. It's something I've used in my own therapy at times." He smiled. "That's if you don't mind being my patient again for a short while?"

"I can manage that."

They started immediately, Anna not wanting to waste any more time than necessary. She needed to master this technique, to emulate Vito Golini, even though she had no real idea how it would, ultimately, help Emily. It would, nevertheless, be a start. A step forward out of the current quagmire.

The lessons in meditation, in channeling energy, went on late into the evening, accompanied by an almost overwhelming quantity of tea and coffee. They kept going until both of them were so tired they began making mistakes or, in Kenneth's case, falling asleep mid-sentence.

Anna made her decision quickly, allowing no time for doubt.

"You should stay the night," she said, almost immediately wishing she had explained it better, made it less of an invitation to who-knew-what. "I mean, you're tired and not in a fit state to drive anywhere. So, you can sleep on the couch, if you want? You know, that's what I meant. You…on the couch."

Kenneth nodded, smiling. "Absolutely. On the couch. I didn't for one moment think anything else."

Is he being sarcastic? Anna could not be sure, but she suspected it.

She showed him where the spare blankets and pillows were and left him to make himself comfortable. Even so, it was with a small *frisson* of excitement that she got into her nightdress and settled into bed that night, knowing he was out there, so close.

She was smiling as she settled down to sleep.

* * *

That was the night Emily tried to kill her abuser.

Anna, woken by some instinct that told her the wall had come to life, watched in horrified silence as the man stripped off his clothes and Emily pulled a knife from beneath the edge of the mattress.

The first stab caught the man in the arm, the blade sliding deep. Emily pulled it free to stab again as the blood began to flow.

Anna dared to hope that this would be the end of the man, the end of Emily's suffering at his hands. But he was fast and reacted immediately to the first flash of pain in his arm.

He turned and grabbed Emily's wrist. For a brief moment, they struggled and, although Anna could hear no sound, in her head, she imagined the screaming, the shouting. Once the man had hold of Emily, it was obvious he would overpower her. He was too strong. Anna's heart sank as he pinned Emily to the bed. He squeezed her wrist. The knife fell from her fingers, sliding and skipping across the bedroom floor to lie against the wall.

Right in front of Anna's eyes, it lay as a bloody reminder

of what might have been had Emily been faster or stronger.

The man began to beat Emily viciously, and Anna turned away, crying, shouting her frustration into the dark.

Kenneth was at her bedroom door in a moment, calling out to her. "Anna! What's wrong? What's happening?"

She called him inside and tried to explain, through her sobbing, what she had seen. The horror that was unfolding before her on the wall. Although he could see nothing but the plaster and paint, he was obviously sickened by Anna's description. He put his arms around her and held her close as she cried.

The plan formed in Anna's mind with a flash of inspiration. If only she still had the time!

She turned back to the wall, easing herself out of Kenneth's arms.

Trying to ignore the soundless violence being enacted before her, she concentrated on the knife and slid out of bed onto her hands. This was the reason she was able to see the parallel world in the first place. Everything had been leading up to this moment. She was convinced of it. It gave it all purpose, meaning.

"What are you doing, Anna?" Kenneth stood and moved around the bed to watch her. "Let me get your wheelchair."

"No!" she snapped. "No, I need to be down here for this."

Crawling across the floor toward the wall, she tried to remember the lessons Ken had taught her earlier that evening. They had been going to continue in the morning. But she had to try now!

She was momentarily distracted by the woman who

pushed Emily's wheelchair hurrying into the bedroom in the wall. She looked scared, panicked, running to the bed and pulling at the man, shouting at him. For the first time, Anna saw the woman not as an accomplice, but as another victim, every bit as scared of the man as Emily was. But she must care for Emily to put herself at risk by trying to stop the man from hurting her more. It took courage and love to do that.

Anna tried to block out what was happening above her. Her concentration needed to be at ground level. Nothing existed but her arm and that small section of wall ahead of her. Not the man, nor the woman, nor Emily. Not even Kenneth.

She imagined all her energy, her strength, flowing into her right hand. Closing her eyes, she could almost feel it surging through her, down her arm, into her hand, her fingers. So much depended on this. It had to work.

Very slowly, she placed her fingers against the plaster of the wall, just above the handle of the knife, and pushed with all the strength she had focused in her hand.

Her fingers began to sink into the wall, through the plaster. She was so shocked she almost lost her concentration and felt her hand being pushed away. Somewhere strangely distant, Kenneth said, "Fuck," and she thought it was the first time she'd heard him swear. She scolded herself. Nothing but her hand was of any consequence.

Quickly she refocused, concentrated again. Her fingers moved forward, *through* the wall.

Then the pain came. A sudden scalding sensation in her hand, running up her arm. She gritted her teeth. She had to keep going.

Her fingers were surely burning, the flesh curling off, blackened, crisp. It was an agony like none she had ever experienced before. Beads of sweat formed on her forehead, ran down her face, into her eyes, stinging them. But it was nothing compared to the searing pain in her hand, as though boiling water had been poured over it, or petrol that had then been set alight. The fat would be bubbling away, the muscles shriveling, the blood boiling into vapor. Even the bones would be turning a greasy black.

Emily. Think of Emily. She needs you. She needs your help or this bastard could kill her, tonight, while you watch!

With an intense effort of will that tore a scream from her throat, she kept pushing. Then, a moment of relief as her hand cleared the wall. The pain did not go, but it lessened, and that was good enough.

She blinked sweat from her eyes and tried to focus, seeing the strange sight of her arm seemingly merged with the wall. And her fingers flexing on the other side, in the other world.

Kenneth was on his knees beside her, a hand placed on her shoulder.

"You've done it," he said, his voice a hoarse whisper. "It's amazing. Your arm is through the wall!"

Anna smiled grimly, still wincing from the continuing pain. She wrapped her fingers around the handle of the knife and, for one moment, wondered what to do next.

Then she knew.

"Ken," she said. "Can you lift me up? Straight up, not pulling my arm out of the wall or anything?"

"Yes," said Kenneth, a little uncertainly. "But can you do that? Can your arm just slide up inside the wall?"

"I've no idea, but there's only one way we're going to find out. And it needs to be quick."

Kenneth stood, bending down to wrap his arms around her, beneath her armpits. He lifted, stopping almost immediately as Anna cried out in pain.

"Keep going," she said, crying with the agony the move had shot up her arm. "Keep going. We have to."

With tears in his own eyes at the obvious pain he was causing Anna, Kenneth lifted once more, bringing her up, with some struggle, to his waist.

"Perfect," said Anna through gritted teeth.

She plunged the knife into the man's lower back, aiming for the kidneys.

Blood blossomed around the blade as the man arched his back, reaching behind with his stick-like fingers, trying to find the source of the sudden agony.

Anna twisted the blade, pulled it free, and plunged it in again.

The man stood, pulling away from Emily, and away from Anna, too. The knife was tugged from her fingers as he staggered back, looking confused, disoriented. He turned toward Anna, disbelief filling his eyes as he saw her hand stained with blood on *his* side of the wall. *His* blood.

The woman, who had fallen backward when the man stood, saw the knife, the handle slick with blood, the blade still deep in his flesh. She lunged for it, pulled it free, and fell on him in a frenzy. She stabbed again and again into his chest, his belly, his face, until he finally fell, a bloody mess, to the floor.

Dropping the knife, the woman moved quickly to Emily, lifting the injured girl in her arms and carrying her out of the room. As she left, Anna saw her glance once toward the hand growing out of the wall, the hand that had helped free her and Emily from the evil of the man now dead on the floor. The woman smiled as she hurried out. Anna could only hope she was on her way to a hospital.

Preparing herself for the pain she knew was about to come, she pulled her hand back through the wall. The burning, while strong, did not seem quite as bad as on the way in, but she suspected that was psychological rather than actual. Even so, she cried and shuddered, still held in Kenneth's arms. Finally, her hand was back in its own world, and she cradled it to herself. It still tingled with a sharp burning sensation.

"You can put me down now," she said, sniffing as her tears slowly dried.

"Is it over?" said Kenneth.

"Yes, it's over. The bastard is dead."

Kenneth suddenly hitched her up, rather than putting her down, turned her toward him, and kissed her. After only a moment's shock, she responded with passion.

* * *

There were three long, worrying weeks when Anna, visiting the wall by the new estate every day, did not see Emily in her wheelchair. She waited with Kenneth, both of them anxious. She was terrified she had been too slow to save Emily.

The thought made her feel sick, and she tried to banish it. It would not go away.

In the fourth week, Emily was pushed into view by the woman, and Anna almost screamed with excitement. Kenneth, even though he could see nothing himself, fed off Anna's joy and smiled.

Emily was bruised, but for the first time in Anna's memory, she looked truly happy. She waved at Anna, and Anna waved back enthusiastically. Then, to Anna's surprise, the woman stopped pushing and smiled at Anna.

"The woman's letting Emily stay awhile," said Anna to Kenneth. "She's even smiling at me."

"Can she see you?"

"No, but she knows I'm here. Emily told her. Maybe Emily's been telling her all along, but she never believed her."

"And now she does."

"Absolutely. Just like you."

She turned to look up at Kenneth Gildersleeve and laughed. He was staring at the wall and waving.

Emily waved back.

The Eyes Play Tricks

It was nothing but a traffic cone, smeared with mud down one side, standing on the shore as the waves first lapped then foamed around it. But for a moment, one heart-stopping, stomach-fluttering moment, Kathy believed she had seen a woman dressed in a black cloak and wearing a red bonnet walking slowly out into the river.

She glanced at the other people on the path around West Kirby Marine Lake: a young family, the little girl throwing stones in the water; teenagers walking their dogs while texting on their phones; a uniformed Care Assistant pushing an old lady in a wheelchair; two elderly couples passing each other in opposite directions, nodding a cordial "good afternoon" to each other. None of them paid any attention to the traffic cone. No one had seen the woman, except her.

An optical illusion, Kathy told herself. *Just my eyes playing tricks.*

She hurried on, glancing at her watch. Rachel would already be waiting up in the town. Why had she detoured around the lake in the first place?

She looked back once, but the traffic cone still stood unmoving in the face of the rising water. There was no doubt it was a traffic cone, but she wished she could rid her mind of the image of the woman walking into the waves.

* * *

"I have *so* got to have that!" said Rachel, tugging at Kathy's sleeve, pulling her back to the shop window display.

"Go on, then," said Kathy, familiar with her friend's infectious, child-like enthusiasm. "Let's see what you've spotted now."

Rachel linked arms with Kathy and pointed to the mannequin in the charity shop window. Kathy could not control the shudder that ran through her, even though reason told her she was being foolish.

"Come on," said Rachel, seeing her friend's reaction. "It's not *that* bad."

"No," agreed Kathy, trying to smile, telling herself she was being foolish. "No, sorry. It's nice. Really. But isn't it a bit, you know, old?"

"I like old things." Rachel slid her arm out of Kathy's and hurried into the shop. "Won't be long."

Kathy nodded, but couldn't take her eyes from the familiar red bonnet and black cloak on the shop dummy…or her mind from the memory of the woman wearing them.

* * *

"They cut the label out," said Rachel.

Around their table, the drone of other conversations, the clinking of cups and cutlery, the everyday sounds of the Latte-tude Coffee Lounge failed to soothe Kathy's discomfort as Rachel held up the cloak, examining it.

"There's some kind of mark." Rachel turned the cloak back and forth, trying to find a better view. "Maybe a laundry mark or something. Very faint, but it's there."

Despite a growing sense of unease, Kathy was intrigued and leaned across to get a closer look.

The mark was faded, but the word "Nursing" was reasonably clear, and the following letter resembled an "h."

"Nursing home?" she said, glancing up at her friend.

"That's the easy one," said Rachel, smiling. "But I can't quite make out the word before that. There's a 'v'… 'i'… think it ends with a 'w'."

"Riverview."

Kathy said the word without thinking. It simply appeared in her mind, and somehow, without her help, found its way out.

"*Riverview* Nursing Home," said Rachel, laughing. "And it's only just down the road as well. Must be from there."

She peered once more at the cloak, squinting with the effort, trying to understand the final markings.

"There's other letters here… 'L' and 'R'? Some old lady's cloak, I bet."

"Yes," said Kathy, unsure where the thoughts were coming from but unable to stop the words. "Old. Very, very old."

* * *

Riverview Nursing Home stood, true to its name, within sight of the River Dee, just two roads past the end of the promenade. Once, in a more prosperous past, it had been two four-story, semi-detached homes, now knocked into one, but still retaining a vestige of the Victorian splendor they once had.

Kathy hesitated before ringing the doorbell.

The woman's name had come to her during the previous night's fitful sleep. *Lauren Ryan.* It was not, in any way, a familiar name. Not one she had heard on television, read in a book or magazine, or overheard somebody say. Completely unfamiliar, but she was certain there was only one reason for it being there, in her head, an unwelcome visitor refusing to leave. The "L" and "R" that Rachel found on the cloak.

The cloak belonged to Lauren Ryan.

She rang the doorbell.

The Matron opened the door. She was a portly, middle-aged woman with gray hair and thick glasses, who was pleasant but guarded.

"Can I help you? Do you have family here?"

"No, sorry. I'm doing some work on the history of the area," said Kathy, uncomfortable with the lie. "I was wondering whether you knew if there had ever been a lady staying here called Lauren Ryan?

"I'm sorry, I really can't discuss residents with anyone but family members."

"I understand," said Kathy, "but I just wondered if Lauren Ryan was ever a resident here? Just a simple *yes* or *no* would do."

"It's the Home's policy not to divulge resident information to unauthorized persons," said the Matron, a note of apology in her voice. "I'm sorry, but I have to follow the rules. I'm sure you understand."

Kathy sighed. "Okay. Well, thanks for your time anyway."

"Sorry I couldn't be of more help."

As the door closed, Kathy turned and strode down the path, frustrated and a little annoyed. She thought that, at the very least, they'd have been willing to give a simple yes or no!

At the gateway, she almost collided with a wheelchair pushed by one of the home's Care Assistants.

"I'm so sorry," she said in apology to the Assistant and the old lady being wheeled back to the nursing home. "My mind was miles away."

"That's okay, dear," smiled the old woman. "I wasn't expecting to see you back here so soon."

"Me?" Kathy was puzzled. "But I've never…"

"Not you, dear," said the old woman irritably. "I was talking to Lauren behind you."

* * *

A quick search of the Internet proved to Kathy only that Lauren Ryan was not as rare a name as she might have expected. The search needed to be narrowed.

Despite the warmth of the apartment and the sure knowledge that she was alone, she could not shake off the feeling that someone stood behind her, peering over her shoulder.

Glancing backward time and again did nothing but prove to herself how jumpy she was becoming. Still, it was strange, the old woman outside the nursing home coming up with the name, claiming to see Lauren standing there.

"It must have been a trick," she said, mumbling as she pushed herself up off the kitchen chair. "Things like this are always tricks."

She stretched, yawned, and smiled.

"I'm getting as mad as that old woman. It's not a good sign, talking to yourself."

"Then talk to me."

The voice was a breath, a soft susurration by her ear, and she turned, startled, to see nothing but her empty apartment. She stumbled against the leg of the kitchen table, grabbed at empty air, and fell, catching her head on the table corner and collapsing, unconscious, to the floor.

* * *

"You had us worried there for a while," said Rachel, tucking the duvet around Kathy, who, lying in bed, tried to focus through the pounding of her head.

"Us? Who's us?"

"Me and Doctor James," said Rachel. "Don't you remember the doctor being here?"

"No, not really."

"Anyway, the good news is that the wound's not too deep, and the pain killers he gave you should kick in any time now."

"How are you here? I mean..." Kathy closed her eyes,

pressed her hand to her forehead, and hoped it would somehow ease the pain. "I don't know *what* I mean."

"You don't remember phoning me? Saying you'd fallen?"

Kathy shook her head, wincing as the movement stabbed a moment of extra sharp pain through her.

Rachel smiled. "You really were out of it, weren't you. You phoned, and I called the doctor. You sounded terrible."

"How do you mean?"

"All sort of breathy, whispery, like you could hardly talk. That's why I thought I'd better phone Doctor James straight away and meet him here."

The memory of a soft, whispering voice returned to Kathy, confusing her, scaring her.

"There's no need to frightened."

The sibilant voice was at her ear again, and she jumped, twisting her head to look at the empty pillow alongside her.

"You all right?" said Rachel, a slight frown line marring the otherwise perfect smoothness of her forehead.

Kathy, fighting the pain in her head and the fear in her stomach, managed a weak smile.

"Yes, sorry. Sudden extra pain."

She wanted to tell Rachel about the voice but knew she would never believe her. Rachel's belief in the supernatural never roamed beyond the occasional psychic event at the local pub.

"Well, like I said, the pain killers should kick in soon. Hopefully, they'll help."

"You know she didn't phone the doctor right away, don't you? She put her makeup on first, got all dressed up for the attractive,

young doctor."

Kathy struggled to keep the smile on her face, trying to ignore the increasingly venomous, hissing voice. Perhaps the knock on her head was making her hear things? Trouble was, she'd first heard the voice *before* she fell and banged her head!

"You were a definite second in her priorities. Third, if you count making sure she had enough condoms in her bag just in case she got lucky! Do you really think she cares about you?"

Kathy closed her eyes, wishing she could block out the voice. It sounded so close now; it was more inside than outside her head. Tears trickled from beneath her eyelids, and she wasn't sure whether she cried because hearing the voice scared her, or because she believed what it said.

* * *

The old women came knocking at her door mid-morning the following day.

Kathy knew she should probably stay in bed and rest. She'd already phoned work to say she wouldn't be in. But after less than half-an-hour, she had decided lying there, dozing, would just drive her even crazier than she already was. Instead, she got up slowly, feeling slightly dizzy but able to shuffle around the apartment and at least look after herself. Any cleaning could go to hell for the moment.

When someone knocked on the apartment door, rang the bell, waited barely a few seconds, and then knocked and rang again, Kathy cursed them under her breath and made her way unsteadily across the floor.

If it turned out to be a door-to-door salesman, she would not be responsible for her actions.

She pulled open the door, prepared to scowl angrily at the young man or woman selling whatever cheap plastic crap they were pushing that day, and was surprised to find four old women outside. The wheelchair-bound woman at the front seemed familiar, and it took Kathy a moment to recognize her as the person she'd almost walked into outside the Riverview Nursing Home.

The woman in the chair smiled and said, "We've come to see Lauren."

* * *

"When Lauren first came to the Home," said the chair-bound old woman, who had introduced herself as Felicity Baxter, Fliss to her friends, "she read a few palms, did the Tarot, basic fortune-telling stuff."

Her wheelchair was tucked safely alongside the couch, where the other three women sat. They all sipped cups of tea made by Kathy, who sat opposite them, fascinated despite her initial surprise.

"Later on," said Fliss, "it got a bit more serious."

"Serious?" Kathy held her own mug of tea cupped in her hands. The ache in her head was still there but was, for the moment at least, pushed into the background. "You mean like Ouija board, séances, that kind of thing?"

"Not really," said Fliss, glancing toward the other women, who all nodded at her to continue. "Lauren wasn't into contacting the dead, doing all that Medium stuff. What she did was cast spells."

Kathy smiled despite herself, unable to suppress the reaction. "What was she? Some kind of white witch?"

Fliss and the other ladies did not smile, looking grim and serious.

"Oh, she was a witch all right," said Fliss, nodding. "But there was nothing *white* about Lauren's witchcraft."

Kathy and the old women stared at each other in silence, Kathy unsure what to say, the old women waiting to see her reaction. Kathy no longer felt the urge to smile. The cold fear that had settled in her stomach told her to take these old women seriously, no matter how far-fetched it might seem. After all, was it any more far-fetched than hearing a voice whispering in your ear when there was nobody there?

"But why…" She stopped, knowing the question she wanted to ask but unsure she really wanted the answer. "Why have you all come here?"

"I'm a bit muddled in the head these days," said Fliss. "When I saw you the other day outside the home, Lauren was standing behind you. Took me 'til a while afterward to remember that she was dead. Then it was obvious. Lauren's spirit has attached itself to you."

The fear in Kathy's stomach rolled, ground into her, made her nauseous. Even so, there was a question she had to ask.

"How did she die?"

Fliss glanced at the other women, and they smiled, nodding at her.

"It was all planned," said Fliss. "Lauren's body, like all of ours, was old, worn out. She planned to be reborn, said that once she had done it, she would help the rest of us to do the same."

"Reborn? You mean reincarnation?"

"No, dear, not reincarnation. Reborn. Taking over a younger body, combining the strength of youth with her power. Once she had that, she said she would be able to do anything, and we would be young again, too!"

The gleam of fanaticism in the old woman's eyes unsettled Kathy, and she began to wish she had never invited them all inside. But they had seemed so harmless, if a little strange. Now she was not so sure.

"She walked into the river, giving up her old body to await the right replacement," continued Fliss. "She stepped off the pathway just along from here and walked straight out into the water."

Kathy was stunned as she remembered the vision she had seen, the traffic cone that had become a woman in cloak and bonnet walking into the waves.

"I saw her," she gasped, more to herself than the women with her. "I saw her just a few days ago, walking out into the river."

Fliss and the others laughed.

"You see?" said the woman in the chair. "I knew you were the Chosen One. Lauren has chosen you, shown you her death, led you to her cloak heavy with spells and incantations, prepared for this moment."

"What?" Kathy's head was spinning. She was finding it difficult to follow what was being said. Spells? Incantations?

Cloak? "I don't understand."

Her dizziness was returning, and she sat back in the chair, dropping her mug of tea onto the floor, clutching her head to try and stop the increasing pain.

"Put on the cloak, Kathy, dear," said Fliss, and the other old women joined in, almost a chant.

"Put on the cloak. Put on the cloak."

"But I didn't buy the cloak," screamed Kathy as her head felt ready to split open with the pain of her wound and the oddly increasing volume of the old women's chant. "I didn't buy it! Rachel did."

She lost consciousness, her last memory the women's chant failing, falling into disarray, and Fliss uttering one word that echoed how Kathy felt.

"Bugger!"

* * *

She regained consciousness on the floor of an empty apartment. The old women had gone.

It was late. The sun was low in the sky, and a gloom had overlaid the view from the window. How long had she been out? Must have been a few hours. What had happened?

Unsteadily, she pulled herself up into the chair, her head pounding even more than it had that morning, the room wavering, getting ready to spin. She closed her eyes, tried to calm herself.

The women. She remembered the old women. Fliss in the wheelchair. Stories about witchcraft. Something about a cloak. *Put on the cloak.*

Cautiously, she opened her eyes again, let the room settle into near stability. Had the women taken anything? Done anything? The apartment looked fine, nothing missing, nothing out of place. Except the mess on the coffee table.

It looked as though the contents of her handbag had been tipped out onto the table-top. Most of it, her unopened purse, small emergency makeup kit, various bits of paper she picked up here and there, were in a small pile in the center, but her phone and her address book had been put to one side. The book lay open at "R." She picked up her phone, unlocked it, and found it on Contacts, also "R."

Rachel!

Rachel had the cloak. Had she said that? Had she let the old women know? Shit! She had to warn Rachel.

"There's no need to worry."

The voice hissed at her back, making her shift suddenly forward in surprise, falling off the chair onto her knees.

She glanced behind her, but there was no one there. She hadn't really expected there to be. She felt sick.

"Leave me alone." Her voice was pleading rather than angry. She did not have the strength to be angry. "I've done nothing to you. Rachel has done nothing. Let me save my friend."

"Rachel is safe. You are my Chosen One. You should wear the cloak. My followers are waiting for you."

"Where?" Kathy fought to hold back tears. She did not want to cry, would not show such weakness even in the face of this ghostly evil.

"Where?"

The voice laughed, a rattling, deathly laugh that held no humor.

"Why, where I died, of course."

* * *

Kathy rang Rachel's mobile as she hurried out of the apartment. There was no answer. It couldn't be true, could it? She was imagining things, hallucinating. Disembodied voices, old women from a nursing home part of some witches' coven. That bang on her head must have been worse than she thought. None of it could be true.

So why was she running out of her apartment, fully intending to hurry down the promenade to the far end of the lake where she had mistaken the traffic cone for a woman in a cloak? If it wasn't because she believed her friend was in danger and would be there, why?

And had she really been mistaken? Or had she seen a vision, a quick flash from the past showing Lauren Ryan walking out into the river, committing suicide so she could return in a younger body. *Her* younger body!

She ran along the promenade, ignoring the strange looks from elderly couples strolling hand in hand, watching the sunset, the sky red over Hilbre Island.

Either her best friend's life was in danger, or she was going crazy. She couldn't risk making the wrong choice. She couldn't risk even the possibility that her friend might die.

There were old women everywhere, looking at her, staring, laughing. Was that eagerness in their faces? She had to be imagining it. They couldn't all be part of Lauren Ryan's coven, could they?

She ran past the site of the old swimming baths on the right, the wine bar on the left. The water in the lake was unusually disturbed, rolled over by the incoming high tide, waves breaking against the lake wall, spray splashing at her feet.

She could see them! The old ladies gathered at the far end by the slipway, and in the middle of them…

"Rachel?"

She drew closer, her pace slowing as the women turned toward her.

"Rachel!" she shouted. Her friend, dressed in the black cloak and red bonnet, did not respond, a glazed look in her eyes as she stared at the rising water. "What have you done to her?"

Fliss trundled to the front in her wheelchair, smiling like a gentle, friendly old grandmother. Kathy knew the malice hidden behind the façade but, despite herself, could not resist the calming sensation that flowed into her. She stood, breathing heavily from the run, but otherwise strangely at peace.

"Rachel is fine, dear," said Fliss softly. "We've just been waiting for you."

Kathy knew the way she felt was wrong. Was something being done to her by this old woman in a wheelchair? She could not fight against it.

"Why me? I'm nothing special."

"But you are," Lauren Ryan hissed at her ear. *"Only you saw the vision of my impending death. Anyone could have seen it, but only you did. You have the gift. You will be perfect as my new body."*

Kathy found she could not resist as two of the old ladies came forward, took her by the arms, and led her toward Rachel.

"Rachel," she mumbled, unable to even raise her voice. "Please, help me."

Rachel lifted her head and looked at her, but the eyes were glazed, empty of any recognition. Drugged? Hypnotized? Under a spell? The reason didn't matter; only the fact that Kathy knew there would be no help from her friend.

"That's it," whispered the disembodied voice of Lauren Ryan, rising and falling in a soft, lilting, singsong fashion that dulled Kathy's senses even further. *"No need to resist. Just let my ladies help you."*

The voice was right. There was no need to resist; Kathy realized that now. Of course, she wanted to put on the cloak and bonnet and help Lauren return to life. There was nothing in her own life that she couldn't leave behind. Nothing worth living for. Her best friend seemed happy to help the old ladies. Why delay?

She lifted her arms, helping as the cloak was taken from Rachel and slipped over her shoulders. She smiled as the bonnet was placed on her head; she felt an odd tingle through her scalp and across her back as though the clothes exuded some power of their own.

"Now, enter the river, Kathy. Let the water take you and return me to life and youth!"

The waves lapped at the end of the slipway as Kathy, no longer accompanied by any of the old ladies, walked slowly, smiling, toward gray oblivion.

The first touch of water on her toes, around her ankles, was cold, but as she walked farther out and the waves rolled around her calves, her knees, her thighs, she felt an inner warmth. This was right. It was the only thing left in her life worth doing. Her place in the world was worthless. Only by giving it up to Lauren could she have some importance, some validity in her life.

The River Dee closed about her stomach, waves slapping against her breasts, her throat. The cloak floated on the surface behind her, undulating with the rise and fall of the water. She tasted salt, unresisting as the gray river rose over her chin, poured into her mouth, her lungs...

There was shouting somewhere behind her, car doors slamming, scuffling, but she did not care. All that mattered was letting the vehicle of her release, of her sacrifice for Lauren, fill her lungs, cover her nose, her eyes.

Splashing. Shouting. Hands grabbing her. Pulling as blackness closed around her.

And then she was spluttering, vomiting up water. Concrete pressed against her cheek. Hands pressing, hurting. More water forced from her, exploding from her mouth, streaming from her nose. Eyes stinging. And then, thankfully, the blackness once again, and nothing else mattered.

* * *

"How are you feeling?"

Doctor James sat on the edge of the bed, holding her hand as she slowly regained consciousness. Her throat was sore, her whole body aching.

"Good to see you awake again," said Rachel, standing behind the doctor, her smile not completely hiding her concern.

"What…" Kathy's voice cracked, her throat scratching painfully. She coughed, tried again. "What happened?"

"Remember that stupid cloak and bonnet I bought?" said Rachel, shifting feet with some discomfort at her confession. "Seems they belonged to some crazy old woman, and these other crazy old ladies believed she was some kind of witch. I don't really remember much." Her eyes glazed over as she tried to recall the events. "The police say I was drugged or something, but… well… Doctor James here spoke more to the police than I did. He wasn't stoned."

"These old women," said Doctor James, smiling with an easy, intimate bedside manner. "Seems they had some idea that they could bring their friend, leader, whatever, back to life by putting you in the cloak and bonnet and sacrificing you. I think you were possibly hypnotized. Seems the old woman in the wheelchair had taken an online course a few months back. I'm just glad I was passing by."

"You saved me?"

"Yes. Pure luck. I was on my way home, decided to cut along the promenade, and saw what was going on. A couple of other people out walking helped me, and between us, we managed to push through the old women and drag you out of the river."

"Just in time, too," said Rachel. "Paramedics reckon you died for a few seconds back there."

"You need to rest some more," said the doctor. "Don't be

thinking about anything. Just relax. You're safe now. You're home."

"I'll make us all a drink," said Rachel, smiling and dropping a carefully manicured hand on the doctor's shoulder. "I'm really sorry, Kathy. I had no idea when I bought that stupid cloak and bonnet…" She let the words trail away, shaking her head slightly as she moved off toward the kitchen area, followed a moment later by Doctor James.

Kathy watched them with keen eyes. Doctor James in his suit, white shirt unbuttoned at the top, no tie. He seemed relaxed; talking to Rachel, his smile showed the dimples in his cheeks. Rachel, in contrast, posed. She leaned back against the kitchen counter, back arched slightly to push her breasts forward, head tilted in what she no doubt thought was a cute way. And was that a pout on those perfectly made-up lips? Really? A pout?

Bored with watching Rachel flirt, Kathy looked around the bedroom. Plain, simple decoration, but nice enough. Could do with some wallpaper, though. Something flowery. Nice view of the river through the window. This was good. She could enjoy this, and the nice young doctor, once she got rid of that bitch, Rachel. Get Rachel out the way and Doctor James was all hers.

So, she died for a few seconds, did she? That was all it took. A few seconds.

Lauren Ryan looked out through Kathy's eyes—no, *her* eyes—and was ready to begin her new life.

Abandoned

The ghosts of the abandoned chattered through the trees as the winter rain overflowed the afternoon and poured into evening. Gunnar and Leif huddled in their rain capes in the slight shelter of an old, broad tree and listened. They knew the sound of the rain, the hiss as it hit the leaves, the rapid tapping as it dripped from branches, but behind the familiar were the ghosts, chattering, rushing back and forth, agitated, looking for something…or someone.

"We'll freeze if we don't move soon," said Gunnar, the older of the two brothers.

"But the ghosts. What about the ghosts?"

Gunnar breathed deeply, calming the fluttering in his stomach. Just back from three years of university, living in the city, he was too intelligent, too wise to believe in the old folk tales of his grandparents. And yet he was afraid. There was no such thing as ghosts, in the woods or otherwise. He knew this. It did not take his fear away.

"The ghosts are just noises," he said, determined to show

Leif that his time away from home had changed him. "Nothing more. Just sounds. Sounds can't hurt us, but the cold can. We need to get home."

"We shouldn't have walked through the woods," said Leif, shivering from cold and fear. "It's Halloween, for God's sake! Everyone knows bad things happen on Halloween."

"Yes, Leif, bad things happen. Kids knock on your door and ask for candy. People dress up in stupid costumes, and the shops are full of plastic crap that's meant to look somehow scary. *Very* bad things." Gunnar laughed. It helped cover the slight tremble in his voice that gave the lie to his show of bravado. "Now, come on."

They pushed away from the shelter of the tree, wincing against rain whipped to a bitter cold fury by a sudden wind.

"It's all right for you, Gunnar," said Leif, following behind his brother. "You got away from the village. You didn't have to live through the last few years. Things have changed."

Gunnar stopped, despite the rain in his face, and turned to Leif.

"The village? What are you talking about? We live on a suburban estate in England, not some rural hamlet in medieval Norway. Our grandparents may have been born back there, but everyone since is English, born and bred."

"But I'm telling you things have changed," insisted Leif. "It's not just the grandparents. Everyone is talking about the old ways and how things are returning to them. Even Missus Dahlby at number 58 has stopped going to church on Sunday, and you know what she was like with her Virgin Mary statues and crucifixes all over the place. She's gone back to worshipping the old gods. They all have."

Gunnar hesitated. He could see the genuine worry, even fear, in his brother's eyes, and yet he could not believe that a whole community on a housing estate could throw off the civilized ways of the modern world and return to barbaric, earlier beliefs. He'd noticed nothing when he returned home the previous week, except that, now he came to think about it, the small crucifix that his mother always kept on the sideboard "just in case a prayer was needed" was not there. And Sunday morning had been extremely quiet. None of the usual car doors slamming as people drove off to church.

"Come on," he said to Leif, determined to ensure his civilized and educated way of thinking would not be overwhelmed by superstition and folklore. "Let's just get home."

"Coming through the woods was a mistake."

"Well, to be fair, we didn't know it was going to pour down then."

"No! I mean, the woods aren't safe."

Gunnar once again saw the fear in his brother's eyes. He struggled to believe that the carefree, confident teenager he had left three years ago had become the frightened, superstitious, *gullible* person before him now.

"How do you mean not safe?" he said, hoping that he could calm Leif down by getting him to talk, explain. Then it might be possible to put all these irrational fears to rest.

"Can't you hear the ghosts in the trees?"

"I hear wind and rain and all sorts of other noises you would expect in the woods on a rainy night," sighed Gunnar. "There are no ghosts."

"I can hear them talking," said Leif. "Whatever you say, I can hear them. They're calling the *Mylings*, the *Utburd*, to jump on our backs and make us carry them to the graveyard."

"You're talking the kind of old folklore nonsense grand-dad used to tell around the fire on Halloween to scare us when we were little," said Gunnar. "It's no more real now than it was back then."

"He told us at Halloween because that's when the barrier between the dead and living is at its weakest. And tonight is Halloween."

"Will you stop with the Halloween bullshit!" snapped Gunnar angrily.

He paused, gathered his thoughts, and calmed himself. It would do no good to start a shouting match with Leif.

"Listen," he said, his voice calm and in control. "If you choose to believe old legend and folklore, that's your business. But even if you think it's all true, my memory is that *Myling* were the ghosts of unwanted children, abandoned straight after birth in the woods to die. Now, surely you're not telling me that people on our estate have been killing babies, are you? I mean, surely you can see how ridiculous that is?"

Leif looked up at his brother with tears in his eyes.

"Gunnar, until mum and dad left her out in these woods, we had a sister."

Sister?

In stunned silence, Gunnar stared at his brother. Somewhere behind the wind and rain he thought he heard slight, brittle laughter, but he dismissed it. Just another noise caused by the weather in the trees. What else could it be?

"Mum got pregnant about a year after you left," said Leif, continuing in a low voice that Gunnar strained to hear. "It was a baby girl, a sister, but dad had wanted another boy. He said a girl was of no use to him or the family, that with you gone we needed another boy to continue the line."

"No one told me," said Gunnar, his voice cracking. "Why didn't anyone tell me?"

"I was forbidden. I don't know why."

"Forbidden? What the fuck is going on in this place?" Gunnar's voice rose as anger replaced disbelief. "You could have emailed. Mum and dad would never have known. You could have sent me a text, anything!"

Leif glanced behind him. Was that movement between the trees? Something flitting from trunk to trunk, hiding behind the rain and the darkness?

"Gunnar? We need to get out of these woods."

Gunnar ignored his brother as he struggled to bring his anger under control, to understand. It was difficult.

"Tell me what happened when the baby was born."

Leif, his fear growing, his conviction that something nearby was strengthening, shook his head, blinking stinging raindrops from his eyes.

"Gunnar…"

"Tell me!"

Leif hesitated. Was that laughter or wind in the branches? Did something just duck behind the trunk of that tree, or was it rain stirring the leaves?

"The baby was born. It was a girl. Dad got rid of it. What else is there to tell?" His voice trembled with fear, grew high-pitched with desperation. "Please, we need to go."

Gunnar refused to move.

"How did he get rid of it? It's impossible. There would be hospital records, doctor's notes, all kinds of stuff."

"No hospital, and the doctor's from the village. He's one of them. He helped dad bring the baby out here and leave her to die."

Gunnar shook his head, struggling to understand, to believe.

A pale shape darted between the trees behind Leif, the movement catching Gunnar's eye. He stared, and his fear returned, fighting his anger for dominance. He could feel the civilization of the previous three years being stripped from his mind, layer by layer. Desperately, he held on.

"Who's out there?" he shouted, making Leif jump. "Stop messing about and show yourself!"

Leif glanced around fearfully. The voices behind the wind were amused, laughing. "What…?"

"Someone's running around back there," said Gunnar, pointing over Leif's shoulder. "I'm not in the mood for all this."

He waited a few moments more, and when no one came out from behind the trees, he wiped the rain from his face and sighed.

"Let's just get home. With a bit of luck, whoever's out there will get hypothermia!"

He turned, preparing to continue their walk toward home, and stopped. A figure stood on the path, rain-sodden and barely dressed in a ripped and tattered nightdress. A little girl, no more than six years old.

"Gunnar…" began Leif, his voice strained and quiet.

"Don't even think it," said Gunnar angrily. "Our sister would be a little over one year old. You're being stupid. Now get on your phone and call for help."

His voice softened as he smiled at the girl, wondering if perhaps she was the victim of an attack or had just wandered off from home.

"What's your name?" he said. "Mine's Gunnar, and this is my brother, Leif. Don't be frightened; we won't hurt you."

"I can't get a signal," hissed Leif. "Nothing."

Gunnar continued to smile at the girl. "What are you doing out here? You must be cold. Here." He quickly pulled off his rain cape and held it out to the girl.

She did not move.

"Will you take me home?"

Her voice was soft, almost lost in the hiss of the never-ending rain, yet it seemed to echo through the trees all around them.

"Of course, we'll take you home," said Gunnar, still holding the cape toward her. "Where do you live?"

"Will you carry me?"

The echoes were louder this time, causing Gunnar to glance around, wondering if more children were hiding in the darkness. *But that just wasn't possible*, he told himself.

He could hear Leif behind him, breathing heavily, obviously frightened. He guessed he heard the echoes, too.

"Are you tired?" he asked the girl, suppressing his own fear, telling himself it was stupid superstition and all the talk from Leif that was getting to him. Nothing else. "Of course, I'll carry you if you're tired."

"Will your brother carry my brother, too?"

The girl raised an arm and pointed over Gunnar's shoulder. He turned and saw Leif staring, wide-eyed, at the small boy who stood nearby, as pale and emaciated as the girl.

"How many of you are there?" stammered Gunner, trying to recover from the surprise of seeing the second child. *What the hell was going on in these woods?*

"Just the two of us, for now," said the girl. "It's enough. Will you carry us?"

Gunnar shuddered, wondering if it was just cold and damp that caused him to react so, or whether his fear was taking control. He wasn't sure he could tell any more. Nevertheless, he was a civilized man, and here were two children in obvious need of help. He looked at his brother, saw fear in his eyes, but knew he would, ultimately, feel the same. How could they refuse?

"Of course, we'll carry you."

He didn't even see the girl move. She was simply no longer on the path, and he felt the sudden weight of her on his back, fingers pressing into his shoulder, legs gripping around his waist.

"Careful," he said, stumbling under the unexpected burden. "You're hurting…"

Her fingers burned through the polyester of his jacket and dug deep into the flesh of his shoulders, melting into the muscles. He screamed with the sharp, withering pain. The clothing on his back blackened, flared into small gouts of flame, and became ash. His flesh bubbled and popped as the girl's body fused to his.

Even through his pain, he wondered about Leif. Had his brother managed to escape? Was he even now on his way to get help? But then he heard the screams, the laughter of the small boy, and he knew his brother suffered, too.

He fell to his knees, the searing pain in his back spreading through his limbs, into his neck, his head. His whole body screamed at him to lose consciousness, to escape from the agony for a little while, but he did not pass out, *could* not pass out.

"You can't go to sleep," said the girl, mocking, in his ear. "If you sleep, you cannot carry us."

Gunnar tried to focus through the pain, to make some kind of sense of what was happening. But there *was* no sense to the way the girl's body had melted into his, how her bones scratched at his spine with each movement, how her skin stretched and became one with his own.

"What do you want?" He managed to gasp out the words through gritted teeth.

"You promised to carry us," said the girl, the sing-song tone of her voice edged with menace. "You can't break a promise."

He tried to turn his head to see Leif, but his neck would not move with the extra burden of the girl's head resting on it.

"Leif!" His throat stabbed agony through him as he shouted, his voice weak, broken.

For a moment, there was no sound save the soft under-breath giggling of the thing on his back. Then he heard his brother's voice, strained, near breakdown.

"He's on my back, Gunnar… *Myling*… Lord, help me… It hurts!"

Myling!

Could Leif have been right? Gunnar's educated mind railed against it, but he could not explain the *thing* on his back. Did the old superstitions have some basis in truth? He could not deny the evidence.

"Are you *Mylings*?" He whispered the question, but his throat still felt as though it were lined with razor blades.

"It is a name," said the girl. "Some say *Utburd* in memory of how they made us. We call ourselves none of these. We just are. Now, carry us!"

Gunnar climbed to his feet, roaring his pain out loud, no longer controlling his own legs. The rain strengthened, its hiss answering his pain, two raw sounds of nature crashing head-on in the woods.

"Where are we going?" he said, fighting the flesh-stripping agony of his throat to ask the question.

"Don't worry; we know the way."

He walked, unable to feel, let alone control, his feet as they took step by step through the wet, clinging leaves on the ground. He managed one more word before the blood filling his mouth made him choke and spit and grow silent.

"Why?"

The girl laughed, an almost sweet sound in the dark and the rain if he had not known what it came from.

"Why? To see your sister, of course!"

* * *

Soaked through, rainwater spat out with each gasp of breath, and forced to trudge onward with no control over their own legs, Gunnar and Leif suffered their journey into depths of the woods they did not know existed. The things on their backs, parasitic children, in turns giggled and hissed, spat words of encouragement and sudden Tourette-like outbursts of vitriol against the people who had abandoned them.

Gunnar's faith in logic, in modern science, was shaken. Through the tight tugging of merged skin and the scratching of exposed bone, he tried to fit these things that had attached themselves to him and his brother into the world view he had adopted since leaving home. But they refused to fit. The only place they *did* fit was in the archaic superstitions and beliefs of his ancestors.

Mylings. Utburd. One which is taken outside.

Could he really believe that his family, the whole estate, most of whom had been born in this country, had turned to the ancient gods and were guilty of infanticide? Why was that any less believable than the impossible creature that had leeched itself to his back and drove him toward a sister he never knew he had?

Behind him, he could hear Leif moan, suffering the pain in his throat to mutter prayers, Christian prayers, under his labored breath. For a moment, Gunnar envied him his faith, but he quickly discarded the thought. He would not abandon his non-belief through fear. There were no gods, ancient or otherwise. His only belief was in science, in logic, in proof and evidence. He could not deny that the creature on his back was strange and completely unknown to him, but his ignorance did not make it supernatural.

The melted, merged skin and scratching bones screamed otherwise. It was difficult for him to ignore them.

They reached a clearing, and with the control over his legs suddenly released, Gunnar dropped to his knees, staring with disbelief at the scene before him.

Children filled the clearing, most dressed in rags, some naked, huddled together on the ground or simply standing, staring at the new arrivals. There was a strange buzz in the air, an electrical interference-type buzz, a faulty fridge buzz that reverberated in Gunnar's head.

With an agonizing tearing of flesh, muscle, and bone, the children on Gunnar and Leif's backs detached themselves, dropping lightly to their feet and running, skipping almost, to join their fellow lost children, the other *Mylings* in the clearing.

Gunnar could feel the hot, wet sensation of blood running from the open wounds on his back, yet he was alive. How could he still be alive?

As though reading his thoughts, the *Myling* who had been on his back spoke.

"You will be surprised how quickly your wounds heal. You carried us to our destination as we asked. We are not savages. You will live."

All pretense at disbelief gone, Gunnar stared at the *Mylings* who filled the clearing.

"There are so many," he gasped, his throat already beginning to heal itself. "How long has this been going on?"

Leif, his brother, struggled to shuffle forward to his side.

"I don't think it ever stopped."

The *Mylings* stepped back without warning, opening a path-way to the stump of a lightning-struck tree. On the stump sat a small child, no more than one or two years old. A girl. She stared at them with open curiosity, and a small smile twitched on her lips.

"This," said the *Myling* who had ridden Gunnar to the clearing, "is your sister. Abandoned but rescued by myself and my friends."

Gunnar could not take his eyes off the girl. Nor could he deny a family resemblance. He no longer doubted the story Leif had told him of the pregnancy, the birth, and the attempted infanticide.

"Is she *Myling* like you?" he asked, his voice weak but slowly returning.

"She was still alive when we found her. She is still alive now. No, she is not *Myling*."

"What do you want us to do?" Leif asked the question, also unable to take his eyes from the girl. There was no doubt in his mind that this was the child his father and the doctor had brought out to the woods and abandoned to die. Despite his pain and terror, he almost laughed at the thought that they had failed.

"Take her home," said the *Myling*. "She does not belong here. She is *Utburd*, but she is not *Myling*. She needs to be with the living, with others of her kind. With her family."

Gunnar said nothing but simply nodded. It was the only decent thing they could do.

* * *

Gunnar and Leif staggered through the woods, finally back on the path toward home. The unceasing rain pounded on their uncovered heads, their ripped clothing, their exposed, scarred, but healed backs. In his arms, Gunnar carried a small child wrapped in a blanket. She rested her head close to his chest, and he did his best to keep the rain from her. She was precious. She was unique. She was a survivor.

"What do we tell dad?" said Leif, keeping pace with his older brother, sometimes looking and smiling at the child. She smiled back.

"We tell him the truth," said Gunnar through clenched teeth. "We expose his crimes, confront him with the horror of what he has tried to do. Then we tell the police, social services, anyone who will listen and who can put a stop to this ridiculous mania that seems to have taken over the people here."

"But our parents could go to jail," said Leif, an uncertain whine in his voice. He had never left home, never left his family. The bond was strong despite his disgust at what they had done.

For a moment, Gunnar said nothing, continuing to push his way through the rain, the woods, the pain in his legs and back. Then one word was spat from his mouth with venom and barely controlled rage. "Good!"

* * *

Brander Evenson was sitting in his front room, comfortable in his armchair, reading the evening paper, when Gunnar and Leif finally reached home. Wet, tired, and in pain, they stumbled through the door into the narrow hallway, where they were greeted by their mother, stepping from the kitchen at the sound of the door.

"You're soaked." Hilde Evenson wiped her hands on the dishcloth she had been using to dry dishes, concerned at the bedraggled appearance of her sons.

Gunnar said nothing, pushing straight into the front room, the child still cradled in his arms.

Leif tried to smile at his mother, but it was difficult. Eyes downcast, he followed his brother.

"Where have you been?" asked Brander Evenson, carefully folding his paper and placing it on the arm of the chair. "You're late." He saw the blanket-wrapped bundle in Gunnar's arms, peered at it suspiciously. "What's that you've got?"

Gunnar carefully put the girl on the floor, where she sat, still wrapped in the wet blanket, staring at the old man in the chair.

"We've brought our sister home, " said Gunnar, his voice low with suppressed rage. "Your daughter. The one you tried to kill."

There was a gasp from their mother in the doorway, but Brander said nothing. He simply stared at Gunnar, not at the girl. After several moments during which neither broke eye contact, he said, slowly and clearly, "I have no daughter."

"Then I have no father!" Gunnar spat the words, hatred and disgust in every syllable.

"Gunnar!" cried Hilde Evenson from the doorway. "How

can you say such a thing?"

"He tried to murder his own daughter, and now he dares to deny she ever existed!"

Brander stood, facing his eldest son. When he spoke, his voice shook.

"That girl cannot be my daughter. My daughter is dead."

"You failed, you and the doctor," said Gunnar, his voice low, almost a whisper. "You left her to die, but she lived, rescued by…others."

"It's true, dad," cut in Leif. "They saved her life. The *Myling*."

Brander glanced toward his younger son but made no reply. He turned, instead, back to Gunnar. "That child is not mine," he said. "She can't be. If you really want the truth about this, the child that was born in this house died in this house. Doctor Mathisen made sure of that."

"But…" Gunnar stumbled over his words, caught off guard by the unexpected confession. "They said they found her alive in the woods, where you left her."

"We took the body into the woods, yes," said Brander, his voice cold, unemotional.

"Brander," said Hilde from the doorway. "No."

"He wants the truth, he can have it," said Brander, without taking his eyes from Gunnar. "Do you want the truth?"

Gunnar regained his composure, his anger. "Just tell me."

"We took the body, myself and the doctor, into the woods, to a clearing the doctor knew from other times, other families."

"Other families?" Gunnar shook his head in disbelief. "You're all mad."

"In the clearing," continued Brander, "we burned the body,

cremated it, and scattered what was left about the clearing. So you see, this child cannot be my daughter. My daughter, your sister, is dead!"

Confused, Gunnar glanced down at the little girl. She looked up at him. There were tears in her eyes. She reached a hand up to him, and he took it in his. He was no longer sure who she was, even though he felt he had seen a family resemblance, but she was still a child that needed his help, his protection. His parents, the people on this estate, were monsters. They needed to be stopped.

"I'm calling the police," he said, his determination returning as he reached into his pocket for his mobile. "You're all going to jail for this. The whole fucking lot of you!"

Brander punched Gunnar in the stomach, forcing his son to stagger backward, losing his grip on the little girl's hand.

Gunnar, winded by the blow, pressed his hand to his stomach and was surprised when he brought it away to see it covered with blood. It was only then he saw the bloodied blade of the short knife in his father's hand.

"You're not bringing this family down," said Brander, the gleam of madness in his eyes. "The gods will not allow it."

Gunnar looked pleadingly toward Leif, who stood nearby, stunned and immobile. The younger son turned toward the doorway, toward his mother, not knowing what to do.

"I'm sorry, Leif," said Hilde as she dragged the serrated blade of the bread knife across her youngest son's throat. "But your dad is right."

Leif tried to stop the spurting blood with his hands, but it spat from between his fingers and ran in rivers down his coat front. He fell to his knees and was dead before his head crashed into the coffee table.

Gunnar, staring at the body of his brother, struggled to stay upright, already feeling weak through shock and loss of blood. He gave no resistance as his father stepped closer and stabbed the blade once, twice more into his body. He stumbled backward, his knees hitting the edge of an old wooden chair. He sat and, turning to look once more at the small girl he had carried from the woods, died.

Brander and Hilde Evenson stood together and looked at their dead sons. Hilde shook her head.

"It's sad, but they would never have accepted the old ways."

Brander nodded. "Sooner or later, it would have come to this." He took her hand and smiled. "We can always have more sons."

"But who's the girl?" said Hilde, and they both turned to stare at the little girl who still sat, wrapped in her blanket. She had not moved.

"I don't know who she is," said Brander. "But we need to get rid of her."

He gripped his knife tighter and stepped toward the girl.

Except she was no longer a little girl.

Her face, so soft, so angelic a moment before, had hardened and twisted into the face of a demon. Her teeth were sharp, like razors lodged in her gums. Her fingers, so short and plump, were claws with curving talons.

Brander and Hilde Evenson screamed as the *Myling,* finally home, sought its revenge.

The following short story was written for a private publication, Hell af a Guy – Fans On The Rampage, *presented to the author Guy N. Smith in 2016, celebrating 25 years of the Guy N. Smith Convention. The suggestion was either to write a non-fiction piece discussing Guy's work, or a fiction piece based on one of Guy's novels. I chose to write a sequel to Guy's 1979 novel,* The Locusts. *It is reprinted here with Guy's permission.*

Locusts—The Return

David Alton slowed the car as he approached the turn into the lane. There was no other traffic on the road. It had been quiet since he left Clun.

He sat nervously behind the wheel of the Peugeot 206, elbow resting on the open window, air conditioning turned up full. Beads of sweat speckled his brow. His shirt stuck to his back. The palms of his hands slipped on the steering wheel, and he could feel the unrelenting sun burning his exposed skin. The journey had been arranged long before the unexpected heatwave gripped the country. Three weeks in, and the initial euphoria of the general public had turned to moans and complaints about the intense heat.

In an effort to calm his nerves, he turned and looked at the view. A narrow, twisting brook, scrubland, hillsides dotted with sheep. And the mountains. Always the mountains. A backdrop of stunning color and majesty. The backdrop of his childhood, a childhood that continued to haunt him. But he knew he could not delay the moment forever. A man in his mid-forties should be able to reunite with his father and face the demons of his past.

* * *

Alan Alton watched at the window nervously, shuffling his feet, absently pulling leaves of peeling paint from the woodwork. Sheila would have been shouting by now, chastising him for not maintaining the house properly. It had been nine years since she passed peacefully in her sleep, but sometimes he could still hear her voice echoing around the stone walls of The Granary.

Nine years ago, he had not been so weak, so thin. Now, when he looked at his hand on the windowsill, he could see the outlines of the bones, blue veins standing proud. He had always been slim; *lanky* was a word several people had used about him over the years, but these days he thought the more accurate word would be *emaciated*. Since Sheila died, he had not looked after himself. There seemed no point. Even before then, they had given up working the smallholding. It had become too demanding, physically and mentally. Now, he survived on his meager pension. His cost of living was not high: minimal food, minimum spend on utilities, preferring to wrap himself in fleeces rather than turn on the central heating in the winter. There was only one expensive item on his monthly bank statement, but that was something he considered a necessity, and he waited eagerly to show it to his son.

* * *

The Granary, David's home for ten years, shimmered into view through a heat haze and, inevitably, brought back memories. From soon after the siege to when he left for university, he had helped his father repair most of the damage to the main house and rebuild the old granary. Now, cracked, peeling paintwork, storm damage to the roof, and a leaking pipe at the side of the house told him his father had not bothered with maintenance. The pipe, in particular, bothered him. When they first moved here, water had been severely limited, supplied by their own reservoir. The extending of the mains water supply to many of the outlying cottages and smallholdings, including The Granary, had made people careless. In his flat in Chester, David was still cautious with water. One of many hangovers from his early years in the wilds of Shropshire.

Remembering their old reservoir also brought memories of how Hatherton's, in the next field, had overflowed into it, giving them extra water. He hadn't liked Hatherton, and he was certain the feeling was mutual. From that first incident with the gate, there had been animosity between them. Hatherton was dead now, one of the many victims of the swarms.

He pulled onto the grass verge at the side of the lane and took a moment to calm himself. The pills he had been on since the breakdown were helping, but it was not always easy to tell. He had to fight to repress the growing anxiety. It was twenty-seven years since he had left, and he had never been back. Since his mother died, he had not even spoken to his father. Flashbacks and nightmares continued to trouble him, and although he had retained his love of animals, he stayed clear of insects. There was a lot to be anxious about, but he had chosen this course, instigated this reunion, and he was determined to go through with it.

By the time he stepped out of the car, the cottage door was already open. He was shocked by what he saw.

His father barely resembled the man he remembered. This frail, skeletal man who shuffled toward him, hand held out in formal greeting, looked near to the grave, if not already buried and resurrected. There was some familiarity in the gaunt face, the sunken cheeks, the large eyes with dark shadows beneath, but it was something he had to search for. Just nine years ago, he had seen him, from a distance, at his mother's funeral. He had not approached and had not followed others back to the house afterward. But he had seen enough to know that, while his father was getting old, he still seemed fit and healthy. The man who stood before him now looked ill, cancerous. If David had not known his father was only in his mid-70s, he would have thought he faced a centenarian.

"I'm glad you could make it," said his father, his voice rough, cracking with lack of use.

David took the hand, wincing at the parchment-like skin, the thinness of the bones within. He said nothing, unable to think of anything that did not sound trite or overly contrived.

"Come in." His father smiled, and David noticed missing teeth, others looking rotten. The nearest dental practice was in Bishop's Castle, or possibly the one in Knighton was closer. Either way, there were dentists a short drive away, but it was obvious his father had not visited one in a long time.

"I have something amazing to show you," said his father, as he turned and shuffled back toward the house.

David, following, felt his anxiety growing again. He forced

it down. Surely, once the initial surprises were out of the way, he could settle and maybe even enjoy this visit?

The unpleasant odor of unwashed clothes, old food, and other, less-identifiable smells assailed him as he entered the house. While it was not overpowering, it was impossible to ignore, and as his father closed the front door, David noticed the same smell radiating from the old man. Outside, in the open, hot air, it had been disguised. Now it made him step away.

* * *

Alan was so pleased to have his son home, he didn't notice him step back. If he had, he wouldn't have understood why. He had long ago grown accustomed to the smell of the house, and to the general state of disrepair. None of that really mattered, not when compared to what he had to show his son.

"Come on through," he said, waving at David to follow him as he entered the living room. "There! What do you think of that?"

He was so certain that his son would be impressed that it hurt him to see the look of confusion, and of concern, on David's face.

"It's a computer," said David flatly, glancing at the system on the living room table, and then looking around the rest of the room, at the threadbare furniture, the peeling paint, the cracking plaster. "Dad, what have you done?"

Alan's shoulders slumped as his excitement was overcome with confusion and uncertainty. Not about the computer system, but about his son.

"What do you mean?" he said, some semblance of anger rising behind the anticipated pleasure of this reveal. The last twelve years had been largely spent getting the system working properly, and it had cost him a lot of money on experts and technicians. He had weathered arguments with Sheila about the use of all of their savings, but she had come round eventually, before she died. She had understood how important this was, to them and to everyone. And now his son, absent for twenty-odd years, looks at a few cracks, a bit of mess, and asks what he's done?

"I'll show you!"

He pointed to one of the two monitors attached to the computer. It displayed a global map with areas of differing colors. Occasionally, the areas would shift, some growing, others shrinking.

"This is tracking the movement of locust swarms worldwide, in real time! Night and day, all year round. There's no other system like it in the world. Don't you see?"

He waited, but his son continued to look unconvinced.

"This is peace and security," he said, determined to make his point, to force his son to understand. "This is my guarantee, *our* guarantee, that what happened thirty-seven years ago, catching us all by surprise, cannot happen again. Surely you remember how terrible that time was? How terrifying? I don't want any of us to have to face that in the future."

* * *

David felt suddenly cold, despite the heat of the day. He became unsteady on his feet, his breathing shallow and rapid, his heart pounding. The mention of locusts, of what had happened here, in this very house, all those years ago, brought back the memories, the anxiety, the fear, and the panic with shuddering force. He could almost hear them clattering against the windows, the room going darker as they blocked out the light.

He thought he heard his father call his name, or perhaps it was his mother?

He blacked out.

It was only for a second, but it was enough for him to collapse to the floor. When he came to, his father was standing over him, looking worried and more than a little confused.

"David? Are you okay?"

Stupid question, thought David, *but one everyone asks in this kind of situation.*

He could feel his head starting to pound, the familiar headache following the anxiety-driven faint. But at least those anxiety levels had now fallen back to manageable.

"I'm okay," he said. "I guess you caught me by surprise a little."

"I'm sorry," said his father. "I thought all that was over with. I thought the therapy, the pills. All that time in hospital..."

David pushed himself up onto his feet and sat on the couch. It might be worn, but it was still a seat.

"I'm a lot better than I was," he said, feeling his father needed some explanation. "Everything has helped. But sometimes, if I'm not ready for it, I can get caught out. And I know it sounds ridiculous, given where we are, back at the scene and all that, but I wasn't expecting this computer system, or for you to suddenly mention what happened. I guess it was too much."

"I thought the system might help," said his father. "I know it's helped me, made me feel more secure. I thought it would do the same for you."

David closed his eyes, pinched the bridge of his nose between thumb and forefinger, hoping it would ease his headache. How could he explain that something his father had put so much money and effort into, did nothing but highlight, to him, the sheer number and size of locust swarms around the world? It provided no comfort, no security. It scared the shit out of him! What was the use of knowing a swarm was coming? You couldn't escape them. No one could ever truly escape the damage, the havoc they caused.

He could feel his breathing quickening again, and he forced himself to stay calm. Relax. Stop thinking about it.

He was no longer sure that coming *home* had been such a good idea.

* * *

Outside had grown dark, the night-time bringing some small relief from the heatwave, but by no means turning it cool.

Alan watched as David carried two mugs of tea through from the kitchen to where he sat in the living room. He accepted one of the cups gratefully.

"Thank you for getting the tea," he said. "I'm a bit shaky these days, and I wasn't sure I was up to carrying two drinks. It's a long time since I've done that."

"No problem," said David, sitting himself back on the couch, across from where his father sat in an armchair.

"I'm glad you're still staying over," said Alan. "Despite what happened before."

"Of course," said David, smiling. "Take more than that to make me change my plans."

Alan was pleased, although he did think that David's smile seemed a little forced.

"How's the job at Chester Zoo coming along?" he asked, looking for small talk, anything that would not spark more panic in his son.

"Fine," said David. "They're very understanding. I'm not expected to go anywhere near the insect house, thankfully."

"You always did like animals."

When they heard about David's breakdown from the university, Sheila had been distraught and wracked with guilt. He, too, had been shocked and worried, but he did not feel the blame lay with them in any way. They had done all they could to normalize things after the locusts had gone. To make sure their boy grew up strong and capable. There had been nightmares, bedwetting, but that was almost to be expected after such a traumatic event. But David had grown up well, and by the time he left for university, everything had seemed fine.

David's refusal to allow either Alan or Sheila to visit him on the mental ward had been their first indication that he held them, in some way, responsible. The refusal had all but destroyed Sheila. It had taken as long for him to forgive his son for that as it had apparently done for his son to forgive them. But he was here now, and that was what mattered.

"I'm going up to bed after this," said David. "It was quite a drive in the heat. I'm tired."

"Of course," said Alan. "I usually turn in early myself. Your room's all ready for you. Do you need any help getting things in from the car?"

"No, I'm fine. And I'm sure a night's sleep will do me the world of good."

* * *

He was eight years old again, running through the fields, Black Hill burning behind him, trees igniting like fire totems, spirits of death and destruction angrily pursuing him. And blackening the sky, with hoppers bringing the field at his back to crawling life, the deadly assassins of those spirits. Locusts. An immense, uncountable swarm closing in on him, however hard he ran.

"David!"

His mother called him. Even in his panic, her voice cut through, offering hope he had given up on.

"David! This way!"

She stood at the gate of The Granary, waving to him, urging him to run faster. He tried, but the locusts continued to gain. He could hear them, clicking, chirruping, *howling* at his back, or so it seemed. His mother ran toward him, her arms outstretched, her love overcoming her fear. He saw her. He loved her. He reached for her.

And where was his father? Perhaps down the road, helping Mrs. Emmerton with her horses. He seemed to spend a lot of time there now. Or was he in the house? Yes! David could see him sitting in one of the downstairs windows, not even looking out, staring at his computer screen.

Even at eight years old, in his dream, David wondered what a computer was doing back in the late seventies. It made no sense. So much made no sense, except for the locusts. They made sense. They were real. They were deadly!

As his mother almost reached him, he stumbled over the rotting body of the tramp, Mac, his foot splashing in the wet, oozing remains. He fell, the locusts immediately covering him, biting, forcing their way into his mouth, down his throat, pushing at his eyes, his nose. He couldn't scream. He couldn't move. He couldn't breathe!

David woke, thrashing at the thin sheets. Trickling beads of sweat panicked him, made him swat at his flesh as though locusts crawled as they had done in his dream. His breathing came quick and shallow. He could feel his heart in his chest, rapid. Too rapid.

He concentrated, told himself he was no longer a child. He was an adult and fully capable of dealing with the nightmares of his past, the death of his mother, the obsessions of his father. He tried to slow his breathing but failed. He fought against the urge to leap out of bed. To run.

Run where? There was nowhere to run. He was back in this house of death. He could see, again, Mac's decaying corpse, the writing remains of Pat Emmerton. He had willingly come back to this place. Why? Was it finally time for it all to end?

He sat up, blinking sweat from his eyes. It was so hot. And dark. Where was the moonlight?

He looked to the windows. They were black, impossible to even define their outline, if it were not for the faintly paler curtains to either side. How could they be black? Why could he not see out of the windows?

The answer was as obvious as it was terrifying. Locusts! The heatwave had brought with it the scourge of locusts once again. They covered the windows, resting now that the sun had gone down, but waiting to come alive again and eat their way into the house. They had returned to finish what they had started thirty-seven years ago. And he had walked right into their trap.

There seemed nothing he could do. Perhaps escape over their resting bodies to the car? But it could not be long until dawn, and on the open road, he would stand no chance. What was left? To wait for death, for them to bite and smother him? And what of his father? All that time, effort, and money into the computer system, and it had not seen the danger on his own doorstep.

He climbed slowly out of bed, afraid that his movement might rouse the creatures on his window. His walk across the floor to the door became steadier, more strident with each step. He knew what he needed to do. And now the decision was made, nothing would stop him.

The locusts would not have him and his father, not their way. To allow them that would be to give them victory. They would never have victory.

** * **

Pat Emmerton, naked. It was how he had dreamed of her for many years after the locusts had gone. But guilt had stopped all that after Sheila died. Now they were back, with the temptation, the teasing, in the bath, nipples proud, legs apart. But he was old and tired, even in the dream. He could not respond as she wanted. He could not perform.

She grew angry, splashing in the bathwater, kicking out at him. Anger turned to fear, to pain. Water no longer sloshed; it crawled! Locusts, hundreds, perhaps thousands, filling the tub, covering Pat's welcoming body with a writhing carpet of biting death, forcing their way into every orifice.

In his dream, Alan turned away, retching. In reality, he woke, confused and frightened. It was not uncommon for him to dream of locusts, but it was some time since he had dreamed of Pat or watched her eaten alive! And why had the noise of his dream not stopped?

It took a moment, but the realization eventually dawned on him that the noise was not in his dream; it came from downstairs. Banging, sliding, footsteps, the occasional muttered curse.

It could only be David.

He climbed out of bed, wincing at the pain in his legs as he pushed to standing. He knew he was not in good health, but he was too busy watching for the next plague of locusts to do much about his own wellbeing. He knew it would come, but this time people would be forewarned and ready, thanks to his computer system.

He descended the stairs as quickly as he could, while still being careful. His greatest fear was that he should fall and break his leg or a hip. At least David was here to look after him and call for help, even if only for a few days. Perhaps, with some gentle persuasion, David could move back in permanently? That would be the best for both of them; he was convinced of it.

He found David scrambling through a kitchen cupboard. The trail of his searching was strewn from the living room to here.

"David?" Alan stayed back, frightened of his son's somewhat manic behavior. "What are you looking for?"

David looked back at him, eyes wide with fear, and something else. Something close to madness.

"Can't you hear them?" David jabbed a finger toward the back door. "They're out there, waking up. Surely you can hear them? They're back!"

Alan, confused, struggled to hear anything out of the ordinary, but other than a few crickets waking up as the sun began to push above the horizon, he heard nothing.

"David, there's nothing there."

"Of course there is," said David, his lips flecked with spittle. "Are you deaf? Look at your own computer. It's obvious!"

Alan, one eye remaining carefully on his son, stepped back to where he could see the computer screen. Everything looked normal. Some swarming in desert regions of Africa. A slight speck of activity in Australia. Nothing unusual for the time of year.

"There's nothing," he said, returning to the kitchen. "Maybe you just had a bad dream? But it's over now."

"Of course I had a bad dream!" snapped David, suddenly standing, staring first at his father, and then around the kitchen. A smile cracked the grim line of his mouth as he saw what he wanted, propped in a far corner, gathering dust. "But it was a warning. And I know what I have to do."

Alan guessed what he was heading for as soon as David moved. He stepped back, unsure what to think, what to do.

David pulled the twin-barreled shotgun from the corner, where it stood behind a mop and a broom. He cracked it open and reached for the cartridges he'd already found in one of the kitchen drawers. As he loaded them, he smiled.

"They're not going to win this time, dad," he said, turning a concerned glance on the nearby door. "I can hear them trying to get in, but they'll be too late."

"Whatever the problem is, we can fix it," said Alan, finding his back against a wall, unable to retreat any further. "Maybe it was too soon for you to come back? But it's okay. It's safe. Believe me, son, there's no danger here."

David shook his head. "Don't worry, dad. Don't be frightened." He looked up to the ceiling and seemed to listen to something that Alan could not hear. "They're not quick enough to make a difference now. We can cheat them. Make sure they don't win."

"David, just put the gun down," said Alan, pleading. "It's no help against locusts; believe me, I know. If you're right," he said, hoping to humor his son. "We can find a way to fight back, to survive. Just like we did before."

"We can't rely on the birds this time," said David. "There isn't enough time. It's good I came back for this. This way, I can make sure the victory is ours, not theirs."

"David, please…"

* * *

David fired both barrels. Blood spatter speckled his face as his father's head exploded, but he did not flinch. He stared for a moment as the headless body slumped to the floor, a thick smear of crimson marking its descent on the wall. Fragments of skull were embedded in the gore, brain matter sliding slowly downward like bloody slugs, leaving their slime behind.

Calmly, he opened the weapon again, loading two more cartridges.

He could hear the locusts, chirping incessantly outside. They would have left the fields bare, all the crops of the surrounding smallholdings gone, and now they were crunching their way through the wood of the back door, the wood of the window panes.

His father was dead. He had killed him rather than leave him to the locusts. It hurt to know what he had done, but it had been a necessity, a kindness even.

From the increased activity and volume above him, it seemed as though the locusts had eaten their way through the roof and were into the top rooms. It didn't matter. It would be over before they got down here.

He stepped carefully over his father's outstretched arm. He didn't want to desecrate the remains by stepping on them. He stopped before the computer, his father's proudest achievement, much more so than a son who had suffered a breakdown, who was on pills for life to help manage a mental illness. A child like that was not one to be proud of, even though his parents were partly to blame. His father's determination to stay at the house, putting his family in danger. The obvious—in hindsight—affair he had with Pat Emmerton. David, as an eight-year-old, might have missed it, but surely his mother knew? Then there was the guilt of knowing that the peaches sent over by Uncle Fred from Pennsylvania were, at least in part, to blame for the plague that descended on the country, that killed so many of the people around him. He had seen more death, as a child, in that long summer than he had ever seen in his adult life. It had affected him. It had *scarred* him. And he blamed his parents for not doing more to help. That was why he had refused to see them once he was admitted to the mental ward.

But he had conquered that. He had managed to return, to speak to his father as one would speak to another adult. It was no one's fault this time that the locusts had returned.

The computer screen seemed out of focus, blurred, but he thought he saw the color painting the UK. Hoppers across the whole country. Swarms coming up from the south. They were here. He could hear them, even now, gathering in the top rooms, ready to fill the stairwell, to burst into the kitchen, the living room, bringing death with them. But he would cheat them.

It was not easy, but with a stretch, and the shotgun jammed against the base of the wall, he got the barrels against his forehead.

Shapes flitted around him, shadowy, unclear, but he knew what they were. The locusts had begun to infiltrate the downstairs of The Granary. His childhood home was occupied by the enemy. His childhood had been invaded one last time.

He had no choice.

He pushed down, reached. The barrels bucked, the blast scattering his skull and brains over his father's computer system, blood and gore smearing the screens.

As the noise of the blast faded, David Alton's body lay huddled on the living room floor. The barrels of the shotgun rested among the bloody pulp that had been the top of his head. A pool of blood spread outward, almost touching the gore that oozed from his father's body, each avoiding the other by millimeters, failing to connect just as father and son had failed. Close, but not close enough.

The computer continued to scroll its data, the map of the UK clear of any warning colors. Outside, crickets chirruped happily in the fields. The Granary stood in some state of disrepair, but otherwise peaceful, only a few streaks of blood on one of the downstairs windows suggesting the tragedy that lay inside. A red Peugeot 206 stood on the side of the lane outside the gate. The fields and the forests were lush and green, the mountains golden, brown, and distant purple against the blue sky. The Shropshire countryside had healed itself after the plague of thirty-seven years ago. Not all people were able to do the same.

The Demon of Heathen Cliff

Let me make one thing clear from the start. I don't believe in demons, the supernatural, all that shit. Well, I *didn't* believe, before I went to Heathen Cliff. As skeptics go, I was right up there with the most hardened, looking down on those weak-minded individuals who believed the fairy stories fed them by religion or superstition. I was supremely confident in my position, and in hindsight, more than a little arrogant about it, too.

So, how did I come to be facing a real-life demon, inside a cliff, in a country I'd never been to before? And what did it all have to do with an ancient bishop and a volcanic eruption that grounded most of Europe's airlines for several highly disruptive days?

Let me take you back to March 2010, and I'll try to explain.

* * *

I'd been in Iceland for almost two weeks. I was on a late, wildly uninspired, and, to be frank, ill-thought-out gap year of travel and non-adventure. But that was me, Robert Arason, Rob for short. Twenty years old and traveling on an itinerary created by parents who felt their son should learn more about his family's Nordic roots. But I doubt they planned for an angry volcano, or at least I hope they didn't. As it was, the first eruption shook the ground not long after I'd booked out of the small hotel on the mainland and into the hostel on Drangey Island.

Back then, the ice-capped volcano, *Eyjafjalla,* had never been heard of by the majority of the world, including me. Even after it had sent out a warning shot on March 20th, everyone but the scientists more or less ignored it. To be honest, I was more concerned about dodging the local bird population, which was large and had good aim, and in mocking the legend of Drangey Island's demon.

According to the hostel manager, a local man whose age was etched in deep lines on his face, and who reveled in the telling of the story, this demon was the reason that local egg collectors, of which there were many, avoided Heathen Cliff, despite the embarrassment of riches waiting to be plundered. Apparently, it was the one place left to the demon by some character called Bishop Gudmundur the Good, when he kicked the demon's ass in the dim and distant past.

It was all I could do to keep a straight face, not wanting to antagonize a man with the power to kick me out of the only shelter on the island. But, I mean, a demon that got pissed at people for collecting eggs and ran away from some *hero* called Gudmundur the Good? Not exactly *Hellraiser* or *The Exorcist,* right?

I started to take things a little more seriously in the days following that first eruption. That was when the rumors began.

* * *

"I'm telling you, people are disappearing!"

That was Mark. I never got to know his surname. He was an American backpacker on an extended vacation. And he was getting ready to leave.

"You sure they're not just moving on, like you?" I said, being the voice of reason.

"They're not moving on; they're disappearing."

"How could they disappear?" I said, suspecting that was a detail the rumor omitted.

"Heathen Cliff," said the hostel manager, appearing unexpectedly in the bunk room doorway. "They went to explore Heathen Cliff and never came back."

"Are you actually claiming that your *demon* got them?" I said, smiling.

"I claim nothing," he said. "I simply state the truth."

"Maybe he's right," said Mark, fastening his bag. "We don't know everything. Maybe there *is* a demon out there."

"Don't tell me you buy into this shit?" Frustration hardened the edge of my voice. "It's just a story to frighten tourists on the long nights. It's not real!"

"How do you know?" said Mark, and for the first time, I noticed the fear in his eyes. "Can you prove it *doesn't* exist? 'Cos I can't."

"It *does* exist," said the hostel manager.

"Okay!" That was it. I'd had enough. "I'm going to prove once and for all that this so-called *demon* does not exist."

My anger was carrying me. I knew I was right, and it was time someone put a stop to all this nonsense. People were not *disappearing*; they were leaving without saying goodbye. It was rude but not that uncommon, surely?

"How?" said Mark, putting his bag to one side and looking like he might be tempted to stay. Even if only to watch whatever I was going to get up to.

What exactly *was* I going to get up to? How did I prove the legend wrong? It was all just stories and superstition, I knew that, and I didn't *do* superstition. The closest I got to that sort of thing was the locket I wore on a chain around my neck. It contained a blackened *something*, which my dad claimed was an ancient relic. "A piece of bone," he said. I didn't believe that, but it was one of the few things my dad had *ever* given me, so I wore it.

And then the answer came to me, and it was so simple.

"I'll go out there to Heathen Cliff myself," I said. "And when I come back, unmolested by any demon, you'll realize just how much nonsense this legend is."

By the time all this happened, it was April 13th.

* * *

Drangey Island is made of the hard plug of rock that once blocked an ancient volcano, the rest having fallen away over time. It can be hard on the feet, and cold, too, with little shelter from the elements. The hostel sits on the top of the island because no one wants to scale the cliffs and climb the iron ladder every time they go for a walk. Most of the hike to the cliff, therefore, would be across fairly level ground.

I don't want to give the impression that I was completely obsessed with breaking this superstition. I was, after all, a tourist, and not immune to the savage beauty of the surrounding landscape. The morning I chose for my adventure, I could see *Kerlingin,* or *The Old Woman,* just off the main island. A jagged finger of rock poking out from the sea. And through the mist that lay low over the water, I could make out the edge of the mainland, distant and ghost-like. I had seldom felt so isolated, so completely alone, but there was no denying that the view was stunning.

Wrapped in a fleece coat, with gloves, hat, and goggles, I set off.

* * *

The trek to Heathen Cliff was long but uneventful. The occasional candy wrapper and discarded paper cup were evidence that others had come this way before me. We, as humans, do tend to leave our mark on the landscape as we pass by. There was a rough path, mostly made by feet tramping across the ground. Either side, birds wheeled in the sky, waddled on the ground, and screeched. Always screeching. They left the path strangely clear, except for a random spotting of guano. I kept the hood of my coat up for that very reason.

The approach to Heathen Cliff itself was as unremarkable as the preceding walk. There was nothing to tell me the name of the place. No signage. No tourist information board. Had I not been given directions and studied a map, I would not have known that I was finally standing on the notorious Heathen Cliff. It was unremarkable in every way imaginable.

Only as I drew closer to the very edge did the remarkable begin.

There was a definite drop in the temperature, making me shiver as the deepening iciness soaked through my layers of clothes and touched the skin beneath. The screeching birds became strangely muted. They still cried, they still flew and waddled, and their beaks opened, but the sound was somehow dull, distant.

I had learned from the hostel manager that Bishop Gudmundur the Good had been lowered over the cliff on a rope by his companions so he could bless the rocks. Apparently, Heathen Cliff was not the first place he had done this. But the demon living in Heathen Cliff grabbed the rope and started to cut through it. It only failed in this endeavor because, with some lucky foresight, the rope had been blessed with holy water. The good bishop then chose to allow the demon to stay in this one spot because, he said, even evil needed a place to live.

I'd actually heard the legend before and had all but forgotten it until the hostel manager told *his* version. My dad used it as a bedtime story sometimes, when I was young. He was very proud of his Nordic roots. But I wasn't Gudmundur the Good. I had no companions and no desire to abseil down the cliff face.

So why couldn't I stop walking toward the edge? I didn't

want to go any closer, but my feet would not listen. They would not stop.

Step.

Something compelled me onward. Irresistible. Terrifying. Doubt made inroads into my skepticism.

Another step.

The toes of one boot scuffed the edge of the cliff.

"Stop!"

I shouted, screamed, my voice echoing around nearby rocks before dying in the icy wind that blew over the sea.

"No! Stop it! Stop!"

Another step.

One boot half over the abyss, the other with only its heel on the cliff edge.

"Please, stop!"

My skepticism crumbled. Fear and desperate belief filled the void.

My feet moved again, and there was nothing beneath them.

I fell.

A scream of fear was dragged from my throat and immediately lost in the sudden rush of wind. Heathen Cliff scrolled past me in a blur, the rocks and sea below rising to meet me. I now knew what had happened to those others who had gone missing, and like them, I was about to die, to be broken, smashed. Another victim of Heathen Cliff.

By the time I was grabbed and pulled *into* the cliff face, *through* the rock, I was already unconscious.

* * *

When I woke, the air around me was suffused with a red glow, bright enough for me to see that I lay in a cave, but not bright enough to penetrate the glowering darkness all around. And there was an odor. One not all that unfamiliar to someone who has stayed in many hostels. Unwashed clothes, feet that had been in walking boots for too long, bodies that had slept rough for too many cold and damp nights.

How had I got there? How, on the point of certain death, falling toward the rocks, had I ended up in a cave? Alive?

"You are awake."

The sudden voice, deep and loud, echoed around the unseen rock walls, startling and scaring me. It had a rough, broken quality that was almost, but not quite, human.

"Who's that?" I said, quickly sitting up. "Who's there?"

"It is I who brought you here," boomed the voice. "I, who saved you from the sea and the rocks."

I should have felt relicf, perhaps even gratitude, but I was overwhelmed with confusion and fear.

"Who are you?" I said, standing.

"I let the others fall," said the voice, ignoring my question. "Let their bones snap like twigs, their skin split, their skulls shatter. I watched their entrails wash back and forth on the tide. And then I fed. I have been here a long time, and I am almost ready to leave."

The words ran chills down my spine and twisted my stomach. They tightened my chest, quickened my breathing. Was this person insane? Or were they something else entirely?

"Then why save *me*?" I said. "And why hide in the darkness?"

There was a shuffling and, as I strained my eyes to see clearly, a *creature* walked into the red glow. It was like no human or animal I had ever seen, and I felt my knees buckle at the sight. It was all I could do to remain standing.

Most of the twelve-foot-high body was covered in dark, matted fur, and it was undoubtedly from this that the prominent smell arose. An overhanging brow shadowed eyes of cold gray. The nose was narrow, pointed, and the mouth beneath it broad, full of sharp teeth and dribbling with drool. The creature hunched over, long, thick arms almost reaching the floor. Oddly human hands, with thumbs and fingers, clenched and unclenched, while dog-like paws shuffled along, barely lifting off the ground. A horrible smile stretched the mouth even wider. A long, black tongue snaked out and licked over the bottom lip.

I felt sick with fear and shock from the inhuman form in front of me. How could such a thing exist? And why did it save me?

"What are you?" I said finally, gasping the words out as I tried to calm my breathing.

"Have you not guessed?" it said, smiling again. "I am what you came looking for. Or rather, what you came to disprove. I am the demon of Heathen Cliff."

The legend was true, as I had begun to believe when I lost control of my actions on the top of the cliff. How could I deny it? Here I was, talking to a creature that did not fit any category of life known to me. Why, then, could it not be the demon?

Because demons don't exist?

Looking at the thing before me, the last dregs of my skepticism drained away. Demons *did* exist because I was talking to one.

"It was *you* controlling me, up top?"

The demon laughed, a low, unsettling chuckle that seemed to rumble around the stone.

"It was."

"You made me walk over the edge."

"As I have done with so many others before."

"But I'm alive."

The demon seemed to hesitate. The smile dropped. The gray eyes, like shards of ice, glared at me.

"I recognized you," it said. "I could not kill you."

"Recognized me?"

I felt light-headed. I suspected I might be swaying in place, but I could not be sure.

"You are Gudmundur the Good, or at least you are of his stock," said the demon. "From you, I have this small place to dwell. I could not send you to your death. Unfortunately, I did not recognize you until after I had stepped you over the edge."

"But I'm not…"

I stopped, thinking, wondering. All those bedtime stories about Gudmundur. The supposed holy relic in the locket around my neck. The insistence that Drangey Island should be on my itinerary in this gap year. Could Gudmundur the Good be an ancestor of mine? Had dad traced our family tree back to the thirteenth century and seen the connection?

Had I been set up?

"Why are you killing again?" I said, wanting to draw attention away from talk of Gudmundur. And it was a question I needed to ask. No one had been killed on Drangey Island for many years, from what the hostel manager told me. What had roused the demon now?

"The rocks are restless," the demon said, shuffling a little closer to me. "They want to spit their lifeblood out onto the surface. It has been too long, and humans have done much damage. The rocks want to remind men that they are here."

"And what do you have to do with the rocks?" I said, surprised at my own calmness. A sense of finality, of fate, had fallen across me. There was nothing I could do but learn what I was able.

I barely noticed the locket growing warmer around my neck.

The demon laughed its deep chuckle again.

"I live in rock," it said. "I come and go through rock as I please. I am of the rock, and the rock is of me. The rocks are restless, and so am I."

It moved closer to me, and I backed away, finding there was a solid wall of hard, sharp rock behind me. I could retreat no further. The demon continued to move closer as it talked. The locket grew warmer.

"I will blow open every crack, every fissure, every cave mouth and mountain top. My breath shall blacken the skies, and the lifeblood shall flow over all man has made."

"Destroying the hostel won't be that much of a loss," I

said, trying to be brave, to laugh in the face of danger when all I wanted to do was cry. I could smell breath of sulfur and brimstone as the demon drew nearer and nearer, overpowering the unwashed, musty smell of its body. It was all I could do to keep my eyes open. I wanted to shut out the world in the hope that everything would go away.

"I do not talk of this pathetic island," said the demon, so close now that it whispered. "I talk of the great land beyond. The mountains shall explode while caves and fissures spew forth the lifeblood. And once that place is no more, I will spread the destruction throughout the human world."

"Gudmundur… *I* gave you this place to live." It was a desperate gamble, but I could see no further harm being caused by buying into the demon's conviction of my identity.

"The rocks are restless," it said again. "I am restless. This place is too small for me now. I need the world."

The locket had grown hot, too hot for me to ignore. I reached into my shirt and pulled it clear of my neck, the thin chain snapping easily. It glowed red-hot in my hand but did not burn me, even though the heat was intense and pinpricks of sweat speckled my brow.

"What is that?" said the demon, staring at the glowing locket with curiosity and, perhaps, a little fear.

"It's a relic," I said. "Something my dad gave to me. I thought it was rubbish, but now I'm not so sure."

I opened the locket and saw the blackened bone within glowing white. A burst of hot air was released as I flipped the catch.

The demon backed away.

"I feel its power," it said. "What is that thing that glows so bright?"

"It's a bone," I said, my mind racing. Sweat trickled down my face, dripped from my nose and chin, stuck my shirt to my back. But still, the locket did not burn me. "A relic."

As I stood there, holding up the shining locket, belief flooded through me. I was suddenly certain. I had no doubt.

"It's a bone from the remains of my ancestor, Gudmundur," I said. "This time we will stop you for good."

I don't know how I knew what to do or when to do it. Like on the cliff top, my actions were not under my control. But this time, I had no fear. Did I consider my own fate, my own life? What am I when compared to the whole of mankind?

I walked to the demon, threw my arms wide, and embraced it as best I could, pressing the white-hot bone into its flesh.

The demon did not try to throw me off, did not struggle at all. I think, in some strange way, it accepted its fate, just as it had accepted that it could not allow Gudmundur, or one of his descendants, to fall to his death. There was a connection between the demon and Gudmundur that neither could break. One was drawn to the other, as I had been drawn and pushed toward Iceland, toward Drangey Island, and toward Heathen Cliff.

The demon and I *exploded*.

There is no other way to describe the sudden outpouring of energy from the bone within the locket that destroyed the physical forms of the demon and myself. Our bodies were vaporized, the shock waves running through the rocks, through the seabed, to the mainland.

Eyjafjalla erupted, taking no lives but causing that major disruption to Europe's airlines I mentioned at the start. You might remember the newspaper headlines. It was a small price to pay for stopping complete destruction.

I was there, my consciousness, the spark that was left of me, rushing along the burst of power, with the demon's consciousness close behind. I was a part of the ash, rising to 30,000 feet, drifting, watching. I sensed the demon close by, but we were both incapable of physical action. We watched. We observed. It was all we could do.

I traveled the world with the ash cloud and, even after it finally dispersed, I remained, floating, watching. The demon is out here somewhere, too, but I don't know where.

Be wary of those small clouds of dust kicked up from the ground, or the grainy feel of the air sometimes when you breathe in. It might be me, or it might just be the demon.

The Failure

The oily, undulating mist writhed within the confines of the pentacle.

The old man smiled, his gnarled hands jerking above the mist, a puppeteer pulling the strings of a marionette. He laughed, a sudden explosion of joy that rang around the white-washed stone walls of the small room. The stained porcelain sink in the corner gurgled and spluttered, and somewhere distant, one of the hotel's other guests flushed the solitary shared lavatory. The old man heard and saw nothing save the mist that danced with the movement of his hands. This time, surely, he had succeeded.

The mist began to slip away from his control. He could feel it pulling, retreating. Like a living thing, it fought its compulsion to follow the controlling hands. The old man struggled with it, battled to keep control, but he knew he had already lost.

The boiling mist twisted violently around itself, and then it was once again free.

Tears ran down the old man's wrinkled cheeks as the mist dissipated, a strangely beautiful shower of sparks floating to the stone floor and melting away.

The pentacle stood empty, a silent accusation.

"Failure," sighed the old man, wiping away the tears. "Always failure."

The sink rumbled, the distant lavatory flushed. Life went on outside the cold, harsh walls of the room.

* * *

Martin Wright admired the close-cropped hair and carefully maintained designer stubble in the mirror. He smiled with his teeth, pleased at the even whiteness. Worth every penny he had paid.

Bright sunlight slashed through the glass panes of the metal-framed window and checkered the well-made bed. The black cigarette burn in the top sheet, courtesy of a previous occupant, was impossible to ignore. He had complained, naturally, but there had been no more clean sheets available.

The exorbitant rate he was paying for this run-down single room left him in no doubt that the owner had tagged him as someone with money before he had even entered the door. For once, he didn't mind. This trip, he was "slumming it," traveling without his usual retinue of bodyguards, advisors, friends, and sundry hangers-on. He reveled in the freedom. Just to wake up by himself, when he wanted to, and get dressed all alone was a rare luxury to him.

The small window overlooked the main street and its

crooked buildings. Most were in need of repair, but they had an old-world charm to them, a rustic ambiance that suited the village and its inhabitants perfectly. The stunning backdrop to this quaint charm was the Carpathian Mountains, soaring up into the clouds, jagged teeth biting at the sky.

Movement on the street below caught his eye. An old man, an Englishman like himself, crossed from the cheaper hotel at the far end of the village to the Inn. This was the man Martin had come to meet. Dr. Ronald Stacy, University lecturer in Ancient History and dabbler in the Black Arts.

* * *

The Inn was one of the oldest structures in the village, its bare stone walls furred by recurrent growths of moss, its paved floor often repaired but always soon cracked and sunken again. Small arched windows, black and heavily shuttered, were the only source of natural light, and as Martin pushed open the heavy wooden door, it took a moment for his eyes to adjust to the gloom within.

"*Bine ati venit!*" The deep but friendly voice of the innkeeper welcomed him as he stepped toward the bar. "*Poate te ajuta?*"

"*Ursus va rog,*" said Martin, his Romanian rusty but serviceable.

He paid for his beer, lifted the generously filled earthenware mug from the bar, and searched for his prey.

The large room was filled with tables and chairs, most of them empty. Mumbled conversations drifted over from a few old men sitting in a corner smoking their homemade pipes. The air was filled with the aromatic, yet stifling, smell of their smoke. He could see no women and no person younger than him. The clientele of the Inn was as old and crooked as the building itself.

He saw the Englishman huddled in the opposite corner, caressing a mug in his hands. Martin headed straight for him.

"May I sit here?"

Dr. Stacy glanced up at the younger man and nodded, sighing.

"Mister Wright. Is this just strange coincidence, or, as I fear, are you following me?"

Martin placed his beer on the table and lowered himself carefully into the rickety wooden chair, smiling, unconcerned by the tired bitterness in the old man's voice.

"You don't look too happy, Doctor. Magic not progressing well?"

Dr. Stacy shook his head sadly. "You make it sound like a parlor trick, Mister Wright. My study of the occult is serious and scientific. I came here to get away from the narrow-minded mocking of your type."

"I apologize, Doctor Stacy. I assure you I didn't mean to trivialize or mock your studies." He took a sip of the beer, wincing at its bitterness. "While on a corporate level, my company has been active in blocking certain requests for funding from yourself, I personally have been following your work with interest."

Dr. Stacy snorted his contempt.

Undeterred, Martin lowered his voice.

"You came here because you believed the strength of beliefs, the superstition, if you will, of the local people and the occult history of the area would help you succeed in an actual summoning of a demon."

Dr. Stacy spluttered, surprised. "I can assure you I'm not…"

"Please, Doctor," said Martin. "Don't insult me by denying it."

"But how could you know? I've told no one."

"When you're rich, it's surprising what you can find out." Martin smiled. "The *why* is unimportant. What matters is that I believe I can help you."

Dr. Stacy hesitated. It was true he had failed once again, even here. What could it harm to at least hear out this presumptuous young man? But the doctor was no fool.

"And what would you expect in return?"

"Simply to be there, to observe, to witness an amazing feat of the occult. And afterward, to learn how to do it for myself."

"Tell me how you think you can help, and we can take it from there."

The chair creaked as Martin leaned back, smiling, still keeping his voice little above a whisper. "There's an abandoned peasant's cottage in the mountains."

"There are many such ruins in this area," countered Dr. Stacy, still unbelieving.

"True, but this is more than just another ruin. Hidden inside is the secret resting place of *Jure Grando*."

He paused, enjoying the look of surprise and then excitement on the old man's face.

"I presume you know who Jure Grando is?"

Dr. Stacy nodded slowly, already imagining the occult power that must surround such a place. He whispered one word.

"Strigoi."

* * *

The storm arrived suddenly, black, swirling clouds rolling across the sky, reminding Dr. Stacy of the writhing, oily mist in the pentacle. Reminding him of failure. The rain followed, a deluge transforming the landscape into little more than a hazy, shimmering mist.

Martin's foot slipped on the wet, crumbling rock, and he swore loudly. Dr. Stacy barely heard him above the continuous hiss and rattle of falling rain, and he continued to climb.

"We should have waited until the storm passed," shouted Martin, hurrying to keep up.

Stacy glanced over his shoulder. "No time like the present. I didn't ask you to come. Once you'd given me the directions, you could have stayed behind in your nice, warm hotel room."

Martin gritted his teeth, blinking against the water running from his saturated hair. For years he had thought of Dr. Stacy as a basically harmless scientist, eccentric but potentially brilliant, investigating the occult with more success than most. Now he began to see the obsessive nature of the man, the lack of care for anything but his studies, and he didn't like it.

"I gave you the information so I could witness your magic first hand. It will take more than a bit of rain to stop me following you."

"So you said at the foot of the mountain."

The young man looked nervously down at the ever-retreating forest and momentarily wished for the slight shelter of its interlocking leaves and branches. When he turned back to the climb, he saw that Dr. Stacy had stopped some two hundred yards on.

"What is it?" he called to the older man.

Stacy waved for him to hurry. "I can see the cottage."

Martin climbed to his side.

The cottage stood on the breast of a hill, a slight swell of rock in the shadow of interlocking spurs. Only two walls still stood, and the roof had long since rotted. The rest seemed to be nothing but rubble, but their view was limited by the rain and gloom of the storm.

"Perfect," said Dr. Stacy. "Hidden away from the clutches of archaeologists and amateur meddlers. Perfectly preserved."

Martin found his stomach turning, twisting with an unfamiliar and unpleasant sensation as he, too, peered across at the cottage. One word appeared at the forefront of his thoughts. A word he was not in the habit of using.

"Evil," he said.

Stacy smiled. "Of course, it's evil. That's why we're here. The lingering psychic forces are always more prominent where evil has existed. Goodness dies so soon after its host."

"That's a grim view, Doctor," said Martin, beginning to shiver with the damp and cold penetrating his clothes, seeping into his body. He knew he had to keep moving, feared that if he stayed in one place too long, he might never leave it alive.

It seemed the Doctor's grim view of things was catching. "How do we get down and across?"

The Doctor, who had been searching the ground while they talked, indicated a little-used path that had become a small stream with the unceasing rain.

"Shall we go?"

* * *

The rain had eased slightly by the time they slipped and scrambled their way down the path and across the rocky base of the rift. The climb up the other side was easier, the path irregular enough that the rain could not fill every crevice nor find a straight route down. It was wet, but it was not a continuous stream.

At first close view, the cottage was little better than it had seemed from a distance. The two walls that stood, a side and back wall, were unstable and little more than shoulder height on the two men. The other walls had fallen, stone blocks littering the empty interior. Lines of stones embedded in the ground suggested where interior walls had once stood, but there was no longer any evidence of the rooms themselves. At a little over 12 feet in length and no more than 10 in width, the whole cottage lay open before them.

"There's no doubt the place has an atmosphere about it," said Dr. Stacy, a trace of disappointment in his voice. "But the same is true of many old ruins, particularly in such a superstitious region as this. I don't see anything to convince me it is anything more. Perhaps you paid your money in vain?"

Martin said nothing as he busily scrambled through the stones in one corner. The Doctor would change his mind quickly enough if his information was correct. If he could just find…

"Got it!" he whispered as with uncanny timing, a lightning bolt ripped across the sky directly above, and the boom of thunder followed immediately, the crumbling walls of the cottage shaking with its power.

"Look at this, Doctor," he said, turning to his older companion. "This is the evidence I was told about."

He pointed excitedly to rough letters scratched into a large stone block, half-buried in the ground at his feet. Stacy hurried over, almost stumbling over loose rubble.

Difficult to read due to a shaky hand and the wear of time and weather, the name was, however, clear to both men.

Jure Grando.

Underneath was a date, *1656*, which had been, at some point, scratched through. Next to it was another, *1672*, and the words *Du-te dracului.*

"Rough translation," said Martin. "*Go to hell!*"

Dr. Stacy shook his head, smiling.

"Unbelievable. Lying here since the seventeenth century, undisturbed. Grando died in 1656 but, according to legend, came back from the dead to terrorize the local populace."

"I know the history, Doctor," said Martin impatiently, but there seemed no stopping the Doctor once he was into a lecture, however inappropriate the setting might be.

"He was beheaded in 1672, and then the body disappeared as far as history is concerned. If this is genuinely his hidden tomb, then this is the resting place of quite possibly the first reported *strigoi*. A genuine vampire!"

Martin waited, ensuring that the Doctor had finally finished. The rain dribbled to a stop, and the black clouds began to disperse gradually. A watery sun forced its way through the gloom to brighten the mountains below. Perhaps luck was finally on their side.

* * *

Dr. Stacy looked with satisfaction at the chalk pentacle drawn on the stone blocks of the cottage floor.

"There should be enough psychic energy here to conjure up anything and everything."

Martin glanced nervously at the shadows thrown by the strengthening sun over the rocks and gulleys around them. It was already late afternoon. He had hoped they'd be back at the hotel before nightfall, but it was looking doubtful.

"Well, I hope something happens," he said, his nervousness translating into short, snapped sentences. "I'd hate to think this trip was for nothing."

"If you wanted a guarantee of a thrill, you should have stayed home and watched a magic show on TV," said Dr. Stacy, equally irritably.

Martin sighed. "Just get on with it, Doctor."

Stacy nodded grimly and seated himself cross-legged beside the pentacle, his back to the scratched stone marking Jure Grando's final resting place. Martin shuddered and also turned from the stone. Its very presence had begun to frighten him, and he did not know why.

Stacy's eyes were closed, and he was chanting, in a subdued voice, words that were meaningless to Martin. The chanting rose in volume until it became a shout as the Doctor threw his arms into the air and jerked his head back, reaching to the sky. There was a desperation about the Doctor that Martin found strangely sad, as sad as the apparent lack of results before them.

An oppressive silence shrouded the cottage, penetrated only by a strengthening wind winding around the rocks and rubble.

The pentacle remained empty.

Martin allowed himself a small, nervous laugh, surprised that he felt relieved at the outcome. He had been certain he wanted to witness something magical, but the atmosphere of fear and, yes, *evil* within the ruins of the cottage made him question his certainty.

"It would seem you failed again." He spoke the words softly, not wishing to mock the Doctor, simply stating the obvious fact.

Stacy glared at him before turning a worried look to the pentacle.

"I don't understand it. There's always been some manifestation, a mist, the occasional malformed homunculus. Admittedly, they don't last very long, but I've never had a complete no-show like this. Something's wrong." He shook his head, confused.

Martin shrugged, his confidence and bravado returning as he saw no ill effects from the incantation.

"It's unfortunate, but you'll just have to admit that you've failed again, Doctor. At least we have made a significant find with Grando's grave. The journey wasn't a complete waste." He did not admit the relief that he felt at the failure. He had no wish to let the other know of his fear when faced with the possibility of success. "We should pack up and leave before it gets too dark."

Already the night was closing in, the nearby peaks nothing but silhouettes against the dark gray sky.

"Nothing is going to happen now," he said, placing a hand on Dr. Stacy's shoulder in sympathy. "It's over."

He was wrong.

Neither man saw the coalescing dirt and dust swirling around the burial stone, the rapidly forming, thin, skeletal figure, its skin like stretched parchment across sharp, angular bones.

Both were blissfully unaware of the figure creeping toward them, lusting for blood…

Immigrant Moon

Alise Freimanis stifled a scream as she ran face-first into a whip-like branch. Almost immediately, she could feel the skin of her cheek tightening, the welt rising. It would leave a scar; she just knew it. Not that she had the time to worry about it, at gone midnight, lost in a forest just outside of a town she barely knew existed before tonight. The howls of the pack echoed through the trees like every cheesy, old black-and-white horror film she'd ever watched on late-night TV.

Why did she have to choose Simon Chester to flirt with tonight? Okay, so he was hot, an amazing athlete, captain of the school rugby team. But he already had a girlfriend, Vicky Banks, and she was a bitch. Literally.

Alise stumbled as her foot slipped into a depression in the leaf-thick ground. It caught on a raised root and sent her sprawling into brambles that clutched at her clothes. Swearing under her breath, tugging herself free, crying at the holes being torn in her M&S blouse and jacket, she was at least relieved that she hadn't sprained her ankle. That would have been too cliché, and being cliché was almost as bad as being smart. She *was* smart; she just didn't let people know it. It was easier in school to be popular than smart.

The howling behind her grew in volume and depth. There seemed to be more of them now. Surely there had only been Vicky, Eleanor, and Rachel at the start? Simon hadn't joined the chase, preferring just to stand there and smile as she ran for her life. But that howling certainly sounded like more than three. She guessed the whole pack had joined the fun. As bad choices go, tonight was definitely turning out to be one of her best.

She ran on, ducking low branches, skipping over more raised roots as her eyes became accustomed to the moonlight slicing through the trees overhead. She was outnumbered, but that didn't mean she was helpless.

Alise Freimanis had been through her parents' divorce, an abusive stepfather, leaving her home in Latvia to be an immigrant on a council estate surrounded by old people and BNP supporters, and more shit at high school than any adult could possibly understand. A few bitches pissed off at her because she hit on one of their boyfriends was not going to be the way she went out.

Tonight had been a mistake from the moment she'd seen Simon standing alone outside the café. Already running late on her way to meet friends at the cinema, he was just there, impossible to ignore. Flirting had seemed the natural thing to do.

* * *

"Hi, Simon, what are you up to?"

She worked hard at suppressing her natural accent, hours of practice at home finally paying off before she hit high school. Teenage life was tough enough without being too obviously *foreign* as well.

"Just waiting for a ride," said Simon, leaning back against the wall, hands in his jeans pockets, feet crossed at the ankles.

Simon Chester exuded a confidence that Alise, always intensely self-conscious, found both fascinating and alluring. A nervous tingle tickled her stomach as he turned bright blue eyes on her. She felt like every inch of her body was being scrutinized, and she was both thrilled and embarrassed. When he smiled, his even, white teeth shone in the full moon.

"There's a cool party happening in Masterton," he said. "Everyone who matters will be there. Why don't you come along?"

"I don't know," she said, hesitating. Her friends would be standing outside the cinema, waiting for her. But Simon Chester was inviting her to a party! How often was that likely to happen?

"I'm not sure I'd fit in," she said, pouting, trying for the cute, slightly lost, nervous look. Part of her hated herself for doing it, but... Damn it, Simon Chester! She had to use whatever she had.

"You'll fit in fine." He put a muscular arm around her shoulders, pulling her in closer, still smiling that gleaming smile. "You're with me, my guest. Who's going to complain?"

"What about Vicky?"

"Vicky won't be there. Can't make it tonight. It'll just be

me and you, Alise."

No girlfriend, just her and Simon. It was too good to be true. Surely her friends would understand? They'd probably do exactly the same in her situation.

"Okay, I'll go."

Her stomach felt a little tight now that she'd made her decision. There could be no going back.

"Great," he said. "Our ride should be here in a moment. Ever been to Masterton?"

"Never. I guess I've seen the name on a few signs but never been there."

He leaned in to her, whispering conspiratorially in her ear. "It's a nice, little, quiet village deep in the forest. Perfect for a wild party. No one will care if we slip off into the trees at any time."

Her stomach knotted, a nervous, excited tingle raising goose bumps on her arms. She'd had boyfriends in the past, but they were just *children*. Simon was near enough a *man*! The prospect thrilled and scared her in equal measures.

She was fumbling over how to respond, not wanting to sound too eager, but also not wanting to put him off, when she was saved by a bright red Renault Clio locking its wheels and skidding to a stop at the curb.

"Hi, girls," called Simon. "Alise is coming with us as my special guest."

There were two girls in the car, one driving, the other in the front passenger seat. Alise recognized them from school and was certain they hung around with Vicky. But if they were bothered about Simon bringing her to the party, they didn't show it. Instead, they smiled broadly at her, their teeth every bit as white and shining as Simon's.

"Any special guest of Simon's is always welcome at our little parties, isn't that right, Eleanor?"

Eleanor, in the passenger seat, looked Alise up and down, appraising her in much the same way as Simon had earlier. This time, however, Alise found it uncomfortable rather than thrilling, and even more embarrassing.

"Absolutely, Rachel. Very welcome indeed."

Alise was sure some private joke had passed between Simon and the two girls, but then Simon was reaching past her, opening the back door, and helping her inside.

* * *

Alise's mother sat her down at the kitchen table. Her face was grim, her brow furrowed.

Alise sighed. Her mother's expression meant this was to be one of her *serious* talks. She hoped it was a short one. She had to go out soon. Tonight was cinema night with her friends.

"Alise," said her mother, her voice soft, quiet. "Back in Latvia, our family had a history, a past it was hard to escape. But this is a fresh start."

"We helped people," said Alise, growing agitated. This was not a subject she liked to talk about. "We did our best."

"They didn't understand," said her mother, closing her eyes. "People seldom do." She wiped away a tear that hung, pendulous, from her eyelid. "Then, when your father and I separated..."

"You don't have to do this," interrupted Alise, hating to see her mother get upset. "We've talked about this before. It's all done. Everything left behind. Forgotten."

"Yes." Her mother opened her eyes and smiled. "You're right, Alise. I'm sorry. It's just that I worry every time you go out. We are foreigners to these people. We are different."

"It's not that bad," said Alise, feeling a small white lie was justified in the circumstances. "Really. Don't believe what you read in the newspapers. I'm fine. I'm not going to let anything get to me."

"You're a sensible girl, Alise," said her mother. "Sometimes, I forget that. Now go, enjoy yourself with your friends."

* * *

The car journey was no more than ten minutes, and for the whole time, Simon held her hand, his knuckles brushing her bare thigh. The skirt she wore was short, but at that moment she wished it was shorter. In comparison to the skirts worn by Eleanor and Rachel, it was almost Victorian! Her breasts also fared poorly when compared with the other girls. Not only were they smaller, but they were completely hidden beneath her conservative blouse. Eleanor's cleavage was impressive and on show, and Rachel seemed ready to pop out every time she changed gear. How could she compete with them? And yet it was *her* hand Simon held in the back of the car, and it was she who was his *special guest*. There was no need for her to be nervous or to feel somehow less than the others.

The narrow country lane they turned into took them beyond the streetlamps of the main road. The full moon flickered through the passing treetops. The car's headlights, on full beam, illuminated the road ahead and reached the edge of the forest on either side. Everywhere else was blackness, deep and intense between the watching trees.

Rachel pushed down hard on the accelerator, the engine roaring as she swung the car around tight bends and raced along the straights. Eleanor and Simon laughed, urging Rachel on to ever higher speeds. Alise clutched Simon's hand tighter and tighter, frightened by the speed, sharply conscious of the danger.

What if a car was coming the other way? What if Rachel lost control on one of the bends?

She let out a gasp of relief as they finally slowed down. A sign at the side of the road said *Welcome to Masterton, please drive carefully*. Alise almost laughed.

Scattered streetlamps broke the blackness. They were old fashioned, ornately designed. Their light was weak, compared to the bright halogen on the main road, but it was welcome to Alise. She felt a little safer in the light, however dim.

Only four or five people were waiting for them in Masterton, standing outside the small church that was the village center. The few scattered cottages they had driven past were mostly dark. One or two showed slivers of light through closed curtains, but the others looked abandoned. Even the church, Alise noted as she was helped out of the car by Simon, was unlit, lifeless. Stained glass windows smashed. Graffiti sprayed onto the stone walls.

"Does anyone even live here?" she asked Simon quietly.

"A few, but they never bother us."

He let go of her hand, flashed that gleaming smile at her, and then turned to greet his friends. Most were fellow members of the school rugby team. There was backslapping and laughter and more than a few glances her way.

She shuffled her feet, feeling awkward. Eleanor and Rachel had disappeared the moment they got out of the car, hurrying around the side of the church, giggling uncontrollably. She felt alone, uncomfortable. The streetlamp directly opposite the church was broken, and the only light came from the full moon, high above the treetops of the forest that surrounded the village. It was bright but eerie and reminded her of Latvia, of moonlight walks with her father before the divorce, and the tales and secrets he told her.

"Alise! How nice to see you."

Alise tensed, recognizing the voice.

Eleanor and Rachel stepped out of the shadows at the side of the church and between them strode Vicky Banks. Queen bitch of the school, and Simon Chester's girlfriend.

Suddenly frightened, Alise turned to look for Simon's help, but he stood with his friends, laughing at her. She turned back to face Vicky, feeling foolish and afraid. This was a cruel prank, and she was the target it was being played upon. How had she ever thought Simon Chester could be interested in her? What had she done to him, or to Vicky, to make them want to scare her like this?

"There's been a mistake. Listen," she swallowed nervously. "I can just go. I'll walk, no problem. I really don't want any trouble."

Vicky Banks smiled. If possible, her teeth were even whiter than Simon's, sparkling in the moonlight, seeming unnaturally long and sharp.

"No mistake, Alise." The voice dripped with malice, with bigotry and irrational hatred. "You think you can come into our country, flirt with our boyfriends, take school places that should have been given to British girls, and actually become one of us? Not a chance. Tonight is *my* party, and we've been waiting for you to get here. The guest of honor, so to speak. Now the real fun begins. Me and my pack are hungry for some sport!"

The word *pack* resonated with Alise. It conjured memories of sitting up late with her mother, waiting for her father to return from one of his night-time hunting trips. Always worried that *this* time the pack would get *him* rather than the other way round.

"Time for the main event," said Vicky.

Her eyes changed, darkening to red, the irises narrowing to slits. Her skin became fluid, rippling, bubbling as her whole form shifted its shape. Eleanor and Rachel were shifting, too, all three broader, squatter, ripping their clothes off, falling to all fours.

Alise ran, spinning on her heel and rushing headlong into the dark forest, knowing instinctively that the cover of the trees gave her the only fighting chance she had. Now they were on her trail, chasing her, stalking her.

Well, fuck them! She was nobody's sport.

* * *

The trees thinned out, and she ran into a clearing, little more than eight feet in diameter. The ground was dry and mostly free of roots, branches, brambles, and anything else that might trip her up.

This was good, the first bit of good luck she'd had all night. She had run as far as she cared to.

She turned to face the snapping of branches, the padding of paws, the howls and growls of her pursuers. Her heart pounded in her chest so hard she thought she might faint. Her stomach twisted in knots. Her bladder did its best to empty itself down her legs, but she'd be damned if that was going to happen.

Breathing deeply, slowly, trying to calm herself, she nevertheless jumped as the first wolf broke through into the clearing.

Large, gray, and angry, it snarled and sniffed around the tree line, watching her but moving no nearer.

Out of the darkness came more, all large, all gray, and all very obviously hungry. They circled, sniffing, growling, staring at her with eyes that glowed red in the moonlight.

They were waiting for something, someone. Alise could guess who.

She entered the clearing slowly, each fall of her paws on the ground sure, confident, proud. Larger by half than any other wolf, standing almost five feet tall on all fours, Vicky Banks snarled and, if it were possible for a wolf, seemed to grin maliciously. Unlike the others, she did not circle, did not sniff around the edge of the clearing, but moved purposefully forward.

Behind her, stopping just past the tree line, came Simon. Still in human form, he held a smartphone up in front of his face, recording the events.

Alise stood her ground. She had brought this on herself. She had broken all the rules, flirted with one of them, backed herself into a corner there was only one way out of.

Looking directly into Vicky's eyes, she took a deep breath and tried to steady her nerves.

She wished she wasn't so frightened. Her mother had known this moment would come, and they had talked it over many times. They had been lying low since arriving in Britain, and Alise was a little *rusty* with lack of practice, but there was no choice now.

"Guess I'm the lucky one who gets to do the first reveal."

Her face changed, soft skin to hard leather, smooth to ridged and scarred. She stooped, shoulders rounding, back arching. Her knees straightened, then snapped backward, pushing her whole body forward. She grinned, savage razor teeth dripping saliva, and held up her hands, nails elongated into curved, silver knives.

The wolf pack no longer growled, no longer circled, but stood, unsure, afraid.

Vicky stepped backward, hesitated for a moment, and then snarled once more as Alise spoke, her voice deeper, husky, a faint growl in the throat.

"My family are *Vilkacis*. In our native Latvia, we hunted creatures who fouled the good name of shapeshifters, who killed and terrorized."

Vicky leaped forward, jaws open to rip out the throat of this strange, new creature.

Alise was faster, her claws arcing in, digging savagely into the fur and flesh at the back of Vicky's head, turning the wolf, pushing her down to the ground.

The wolf snapped and snarled, trying to twist her head to bite the attacker who now straddled her back.

A second silver-clawed hand sliced open the wolf's belly, spilling gray/blue and red viscera onto the grass, wet and steaming. The claws at the back of Vicky's head pulled free, splattering blood about the clearing. They reached lower, tearing at the unprotected throat of the now-whining animal.

It was over in seconds. The *Vilkacis*, Alise, stood astride the naked, bloodied body of Vicky Banks, restored in death to her human form.

The other werewolves scattered, crying in fear, scrambling away through the forest to the temporary protection of their homes, their families, their human lives.

Simon Chester hesitated, still recording. Alise growled, and he turned and ran after the others.

She laughed, a deep, guttural laugh that echoed back to her off the trees.

"Well, I guess now everyone will know," she said, not sure whether to be relieved or worried. "Vicky's not the only bitch in town."

She turned her face to the moon and howled.

"The Last Harpy" is a prequel to my novel The Village Witch, *published by Omnium Gatherum in 2015. It tells how the horror all began, back in the 16*[th] *century.*

The Last Harpy

From the journal of Mr. Samuel Galton, dated October 12th, 1587

She broke free earlier this evening, bringing death and havoc to the hamlet of Byre. *Aello*. The last surviving *Harpy*, a creature of Greek Mythology, legendary beast of Zeus, found imprisoned on Crete and brought here, to England, by myself just three months before.

Now I am out hunting her through dark country paths and mud-filled fields, while the rain pours down and heavy clouds cover the moon.

It is not my fault!

Crete was in some disarray with celebrations after the recent routing of the Ottoman fleet at *Lepanto*, and I, wishing to avoid possibly embarrassing questions from the local guards about my reasons for being there, had ducked through the streets of *Herakleion* until I found a busy marketplace to melt into. The guards had long gone, and my activities, sanctioned by Royal Command but often seen by others, unfortunately, as *spying*, were of no interest to the purveyors of all things exotic, historic, and often of dubious integrity.

The marble figure was exquisite, and I smiled at the seller's warnings with that false sense of superiority so many Englishmen have when dealing with foreigners. How I wish, now, that I had listened to his talk of mystic words binding the demon within, of an ancient evil, a survivor of the gods. He warned me the binding would weaken the further I took the statue from Crete, but he nevertheless took my money and wished me luck.

The statue was so unusual. Beautifully carved in marble, yet a somewhat grotesque subject that did not in any way detract from its attraction. The body was of a naked woman, but with hands and feet like claws. The face was filled with dark thoughts and bad intent, and I don't deny it stirred something in me. Strangest, perhaps, were the great wings folded down her back. The seller told me it was a creature called a *Harpy*, one of the *hounds of Zeus*. The sculptor was unknown, but the *Harpy* did have a name. *Aello*.

Upon returning home with the statue, Barbara, my wife, much more learned than I, said she had read of *Harpies* in Homer's *Iliad*. I do not doubt her.

Now the creature has escaped from the carved figure she had been bound to by those far older and far wiser than I.

Barbara and I had been spending the evening in the pleasant company of a few friends, celebrating my wife being with child, our first. A scream from outside, cut brutally short, stunned us all to silence.

Assuring our guests it was most likely nothing of importance, I walked to one of the windows and looked out to the thatched cottages of the hamlet beyond.

A body lay across the pathway, feet still twitching, heels hammering the ground with a disjointed, random rhythm. I could make out grubby, clenched fists, the rough clothes of a farmer sodden with gore, shoulders that shook, and the head…

There was no head!

Barbara had joined me at the window, and I tried to shield her from the gruesome view, but she was too quick and recoiled in horror.

Her reaction brought others to the window, and before long, all our friends were aware that something terrible had happened.

At that moment, my *man*, Emmanuelle, of African descent and an invaluable servant to myself for some years, hurried into the hall to tell me, in perfect English, that the creature had escaped. *Aello* had escaped, killing three of the other servants in the process.

"It is my duty to re-capture this creature," I said, more bravely than I felt. "But I would welcome any who cared to accompany me in the task."

There was some discussion while I waited impatiently. Finally, I left the hall accompanied by three others, Richard and Jack, both of whom I had served with on the continent, and my younger cousin, Nigel.

I selected my *cut-and-thrust* sword on the way. Jack and Nigel collected theirs also. Richard chose to carry his wheel-lock pistol, a souvenir from his cavalry days. Thus armed, we began our hunt.

The clouds came over as we left the house, blotting out the moon. Then came the rain, in big, heavy drops, driven harshly from the clouds as though by some unseen hand. It was ferocious and unceasing, and we were soaked through before we even reached the cottages of the hamlet.

And there was something else in the sky. Something large and dark, with great wings that flapped slowly, ponderously. It rose from behind the hedgerows and hovered in the air, something that did not seem possible for so large a creature and so slow a beat of wings. At times it screeched at us. Sharp, piercing, but with a low menace. It rose, but always far ahead or to one side, never near. And then its wings would flap a little harder and it would disappear, up into the clouds or down to ground, we could never quite tell which.

It was *Aello*. It had to be. There was nothing else so strange, so frightening, in the English night.

The first cottages we came to, homes to farmers and the families of several of my servants, were ripped apart. The thatched roofs had gaping holes, the stone walls battered and, in some places, breeched. Blood stained the ground at the doorways, dripped from the thatch above.

Jack and I checked inside. Every home told the same grim story. Entire families lay dead. Women huddled in corners, their children still clasped in their arms. The bloodied mess of their menfolk lay in front of them, a futile attempt at protection. None had heads still connected to bodies.

"The *Harpy* has been free only minutes," I said through gritted teeth. "And yet, there is all this death and destruction."

A screech nearby hurt my ears, pierced my brain. A black

shape rose over a nearby field, wings flapping with an almost lazy beat.

Richard tried his luck, took a shot at the creature with his pistol, which almost failed in the rain. He missed—a rare thing for a marksman such as Richard, even at that distance.

"Bad luck, sir," I said, spitting out rain as I did so. "Worth a try. We have to bring this thing back, dead or alive."

That was when the creature swooped in, silent behind the sibilant hissing of the rain, a black shape nearly invisible before a black sky. Richard screamed, a sound I had only heard previously from men below deck as cannonballs plowed a bloody furrow through their positions. The creature screeched. There was the sound of tearing, of bones snapping, of something wet and slippery being stretched to breaking point and then slapping back.

The creature flew back into the protective cover of the sky, and Richard fell to the rain-sodden ground.

We never found his head.

Jack and I were hardened to such sights, but Nigel, although a soldier, had not yet witnessed any action. He turned away and was sick on the roadside.

"Damn the beast!" Jack swore angrily and raised his sword, scanning the skies. There was nothing save the rain and the clouds and the dark.

I gripped my own sword tightly in my fist, my heart beating as though to burst from my chest.

Nigel rejoined us, looking pale and shaken.

"Sorry," he said.

"No need to be sorry," I said. "The first is always a bit of a shock."

The first. He would never live to see a second.

There was no screech of warning this time, nothing but a sudden, heavy flapping pushing the air down on us. A dark shape came in hard and low.

I saw a gaping, stretched mouth, huge fangs, burning eyes. I saw the naked body of a woman, the skin dark and leathery with huge, veined wings sprouting from the shoulders. It was an ugly, cruel mockery of the statue that had been its prison for so long.

Most of all, I saw the great claws replacing hands and feet. Claws that encircled my young cousin's head and twisted, pulled.

Unable to react in time, I could do nothing but watch as Nigel's head, an expression of surprise on his young face, was wrenched from his body; the skin of the neck stretching, splitting; the arteries tearing, blood spurting in great gouts of crimson to run like the rain over the uneven ground; the spine snapping, bone sticking up from the ragged, flapping remains of his neck.

The *Harpy,* this creature of Greek legend brought alive in our English countryside, flew back into its protective clouds, taking Nigel's head with it.

The headless body stood for a moment, as though undecided what to do, before folding almost neatly to the ground.

Jack and I looked at each other. There was no need for words. Either we killed the *Harpy* or the *Harpy* would kill us.

"We have to stop this thing," said Jack finally. "Can you imagine if this creature was allowed to roam freely through the countryside?"

Before I could answer, there was a shout from further down the path, back toward the house. I turned, raising my sword, expecting the worst, to see my man, Emmanuelle, running toward us through the rain.

Emmanuelle is not his true name. His proper African name I find unpronounceable, so I decided on the name *Emmanuelle* to honor his conversion to following Jesus Christ and renouncing his previous savage beliefs.

All the more reason I was shocked to see him running toward me dressed, not in his *manservant* clothes, but the way he was when I first met him, in the primitive garb of a *Nguni* warrior.

"What are you doing, Emmanuelle?" I cried out, shouting to be heard over the increasing ferocity of the rain. "You look like the savage you were when I first took you into my service."

Savage, yes, but I could not deny how imposing he looked with rainwater dripping from the beads around his head and painting his naked, muscular torso with a strange sheen that shone in the occasional glimpses of moonlight beginning to show through the dark clouds. It reminded me of how terrified I was when he first crawled into my tent, unnoticed by the Spanish guards outside, and woke me. I thought I was to be killed, but he had quickly explained, in broken English, how he wished to serve, to learn, and, more importantly, to help me escape.

"Forgive me, Sir," he said, his diligently learned, perfect English at odds with his appearance. "I thought of the creature you face, and I realized that, as interesting as the faith in your Christ is, it has no answer to a situation like this."

Interesting! I suppressed my urge to argue that Christianity was something more than *interesting*, as I wanted to hear what else he had to say. With that in mind, I threw a warning glance toward Jack to make sure he, too, kept quiet.

"The true and tested ways of my people, practiced since time began, may, however, be of some help," said Emmanuelle, his expression grim, his eyes staring with an intensity I had never before seen. "You know I was a *Nguni* warrior who wished peace and learning, but I did not tell you that I was also *Sangoma*, what you might call a medicine man, a teller of fortunes and a caster of spells."

"A witch doctor," I snarled, angry both at his belittling of my faith and his admission of lying. "The Devil's work."

"Witchcraft," said Jack. "You dare to talk of such things to men such as we? Good Christian soldiers who have fought for God and country against your savage ways? We hang witches in England!"

"You are a liar," I said, the anger rising, my face burning with rage. "A man who has used my kindness to his own ends."

"And a man who might just have the way to trap this demon that would kill all of us, Christian and savage alike," said Emmanuelle, remaining calm and poised.

I looked across at Jack, at how he grasped his sword as though ready to strike, at how his eyes were wild, his face almost purple with rage, and I wondered how, of the three of us, it was Emmanuelle who acted the most civilized, the most cultured. Just who were the savages and who the reasoning, thinking man?

I had to go with my instinct.

"Jack, stay your sword and accept the truth that we have been unable to put up any defense to *Aello's* attacks. If Emmanuelle has a different suggestion, I, for one, wish to hear it."

Jack slowly loosened the grip on his sword. He looked reluctant and wary of Emmanuelle, but he complied with my request and relaxed his fighting stance.

"Thank you, Sir," said Emmanuelle, as polite and proper as I had taught him to be. "I believe I have a *spell of binding* that will be strong enough to contain the demon, although the creature is of a type never seen in my own land."

He held up a straw doll, a rough man shape with the suggestion of wings on its back. It was crude and obviously hurried, but it nevertheless sent a chill down my spine.

"I would have been here sooner, Sir," he continued, "but it took time to find the materials for the spell and to cast it into this *isithombe sakhe obala*."

"This what?" I said, confused.

"*Effigy* is the closest word I can think of in English."

Aello swooped in again, the sudden *swish* of wings, barely heard above the rain, the only warning of approaching danger.

Jack and I ducked, slashing the air with our swords. We sliced nothing solid, only rainwater and rising mist.

Another *swish*, a dark shape swept toward us.

I tried to stand my ground, time the cut of my sword, but the beast outmaneuvered me, avoided my attack, and almost casually swiped a claw in my direction.

The touch was fleeting, a barely felt kiss against my cheek, but it opened a bloody gash from near my mouth up to my ear that poured blood down my neck. The pain came a second later, sharp and agonizing. The whole side of my face seemed to burn and sting, to send stabs of pain through my head. I tried to stem the blood flow with my free hand as Jack hurried to my aid.

Emmanuelle remained perfectly still, holding the *effigy*, chanting under his breath in his primitive language. I cannot even *try* to write the sounds that came from him, the low guttural moans, the clicking of the palate. He had not ducked at the attack of the *Harpy*, and he remained untouched, unharmed.

I had no time to wonder at my *man's* seeming invulnerability, however, as *Aello* turned gracefully in the air and dived once more, mouth wide, fang-like teeth bared as she screeched, hurting our ears, vibrating the raindrops into whirlpools and waterfalls.

Jack turned as the creature neared him with its claws outstretched. If anyone could face down this creature, Jack could. He was by far the best and most ferocious fighter I have ever had the pleasure of riding with.

Standing upright, straight back, rain dancing off his broad shoulders, he faced the oncoming *Harpy* side-on, his sword raised and ready.

I sat on the rain-sodden ground, holding a hand to my face, watching the confrontation. I would have helped, but I suspected I would be more of a liability than an assistance. Instead, I watched, my breeches no barrier to the gathering pools of rainwater around me.

The first sweep of the blade from Jack was so fast I almost missed it. Although it did not connect, the speed and closeness of the stroke brought *Aello's* dive to a halt. She hovered, just outside the range of the sword, her wings slowly moving back and forth, a lazy, almost hypnotic movement.

There is no way this creature should be able to fly, but it is not a thing of our world and, seemingly, does not abide by our rules.

Aello lunged forward, claws striking at Jack.

Jack defended well, using his blade to sting some of the reaching claws and force them back, dodging with his agile body to avoid the others. Then he turned to attack, almost reaching the creature's chest with a thrust. He swept his blade left and right, its razor-edge biting into arms and legs but failing to cut through the hard, armor-like exterior. *Aello* scratched at the air in front of Jack, swiping a claw, lunging with her head, snapping her teeth, turning and using her great wings to beat Jack around the body and force him backward. Jack fought well and bravely but found little room to attack, always being forced to defend.

Aello filled the night with screeches. Sword clashed with claw. Heavy wings beat the air as Emmanuelle's chanting grew louder. And always the sibilant hiss of the incessant rain.

I pushed to my feet, realizing that the fight could only end one way and determined to help my friend if I could.

Aello fought through the weakening cuts and thrusts of Jack's blade. Time and again, he struck true, but he no longer had the strength to do more than prick the thick hide of the hellish creature.

I raised my sword and prepared to charge, yet, to my shame, fear made me hesitate. If that most capable of warriors, Jack, a man who could undoubtedly best me in a duel, faced defeat, what chance did I have? But I could not stand by and allow him to fight alone. My sense of honor and the bonds of friendship lent strength to the trembling muscles of my legs. I ran toward the battle with a shout of fear and defiance, only to stumble to a halt as *Aello* finally won through Jack's desperate defense.

Those terrible claws reached out, encircling Jack's head. Even above the hiss of the rain and the drone of Emmanuelle's chanting, I imagined I heard the pop of Jack's eyeballs as sharp talons pressed into the sockets. Bubbles of blood formed at Jack's mouth and nose as the creature, enraged, wrenched the head back and forth, left and right. I heard the skull crack with the pressure, saw spider-webs of blood spun between strands of hair. Skin stretched and split, the viscera of the human body torn asunder as, with a final screech of triumph, *Aello* lifted the trophy of my friend's head and flew back into the clouds.

I swear Jack's headless corpse continued to swing the blade for some moments after *Aello* flew away. But eventually, the body fell, another friend no longer feeling the rain fall on them.

I could not move. I might have cried; I am not sure. There comes a moment in grief where the obvious pain and sorrow is replaced by numbness, and by guilt. I had called for help to deal with a monstrosity that was my responsibility alone, and my brave friends had not hesitated. If not for me, they would still be alive, with hopefully long and happy years ahead of them. I had killed them as surely as *Aello* had taken their heads. And in my guilt and self-loathing, I doubted every-thing I had been raised to believe.

I hope the faithful are right about heaven because if ever men deserved it, those friends of mine do. But *my* faith has been sorely tested. Before me was evidence of a creature from Greek mythology, where numerous gods watched and manip-ulated man. Where was our one God while this abomination, this demon from another time, another belief, killed my friends and threatened destruction to all? How can I believe there is but the one true God when I am faced with a creature of *Zeus*?

I would have stayed there, on that pathway in the rain, until the *Harpy* returned and took my head, too, but Emman-uelle finally moved from his position and, no longer chanting under his breath, guided me toward a small, abandoned hovel not too far away.

Inside was dry, if I ignored the occasional drips from the conical roof, and there was a small table and a rough hand-made stool. Emmanuelle, who will always be my *man* how-ever he is dressed, had thoughtfully brought my journal with him, which I update daily. And that is where I am now, sitting in a small hovel, writing in my journal by the light of a burned-down candle with wax pools about its base. Emmanuelle is sit-ting on the floor near my feet. Outside, I can still hear *Aello* screeching, swooping down. She has already, tentatively, brushed against the roof of this place, rattling it. I think she is testing its strength. She knows I am here. She wants to kill me.

So, maybe it is all my fault. I do not know. I am not sure it really matters.

Emmanuelle has tried to explain what the *effigy* he holds

is, but I fear my mind struggles to fully understand anything. I will simply repeat his words in the hope they, in time, make sense.

"The *effigy* holds all of my power as *Sangoma*," he says. "It will bind the demon for many hundreds of years. The creature is too strong to be killed, but the spell will hold it indefinitely."

"Is there no way it can escape?" I ask.

"Only much blood, sacrificial blood, might eventually break the spell. But the demon will have no physical form. She will be unable to attack and kill anyone."

It sounds good, if it works. But this is magic, *witchcraft*! And we hang witches as abominations and followers of the Devil. Yet I know that Emmanuelle is no lover of the Evil One. He worships the gods of his tribe in Africa, the old gods who have been around forever. And *Aello* is a creature of *Zeus*, the chief god ruling over many more gods in Ancient Greek belief. And my God? My belief? I am no longer sure. I do not know.

I hear *Aello* again, calling, teasing me. Her wings flap, loud over the sound of the rain. Her claws rake across the roof. She is in no hurry. She knows I cannot escape.

"The old graveyard nearby," says Emmanuelle, as we listen to *Aello* retreating once more to the sky. "That is where I shall capture the demon, bind it by the magic of the old gods. My gods."

This confusion of beliefs would make my head hurt even if I did not have a deep furrow plowed in my face. Nevertheless, I did not miss the hesitation in my *man's* voice.

"You are not telling me everything," I say.

"There is one final thing that the spell of binding needs. Just as blood can break it, so blood is needed to make it work. Sacrificial blood."

The meaning of the words are not lost on me this time. I watch Emmanuelle preparing to perform the deed, but it is not something a gentleman can ask his *man* to do. He must step up and perform this necessary act himself.

I am sorry if my handwriting is getting a little shaky. I tell myself I am brave, but sometimes I doubt it.

Barbara, if you are reading this, know that I love you completely, forever, and I will love our child also. If there is anything beyond this life, then I will watch over you and wait for you. I can only hope.

Emmanuelle had his back to me when I struck the blow with the hilt of my sword. I know it was a cowardly strike, but I do not know that I could have done it while looking into those faithful eyes. He was ready to act, to give everything to save me. But this is not a duty I can evade. So many good people dead because of me. So many friends lost. If only I had not purchased that statue. But the time for such wishful thinking is gone. Hopefully, Emmanuelle will forgive me, both for his headache and for this act, when he wakes.

I have the *effigy*, and I am ready. A run to the graveyard and wait for *Aello* to swoop down and take my head like all the others. Only this time, it will begin the spell that will bind her to that graveyard, hopefully forever!

To whomsoever may read this journal, let it be known that, as much as it was my mistake in bringing the creature here, I am the one, with help from a *Nguni* warrior, a *civilized* man I am proud to call my friend, who will capture and hold it. No man need fear to walk by this way in the future. *Aello* will be nothing but a powerless, unseen observer.

For my wife and child's sake, and for the sake of all my ancestors who may follow, I make this sacrifice willingly.

Another swoop outside. Another rattling of the roof. And now *Aello* will be back, high in the sky, and it is my chance.

If this journal survives, then perhaps I have been successful. Wish me luck.

End of the journal of Mr. Samuel Galton dated October 12th, 1587

ABOUT THE AUTHOR

Born in 1959, and preferring not to think too hard about it, Neil Davies writes genre fiction (mostly science fiction and horror, but he refuses to be held to that). When not writing books, he records music with his son as The 1850 Project, and paints pictures of dubious artistic merit with acrylic paints. When not creating, he likes to read books, listen to music, and watch well-made films and trashy TV. A solitary animal by nature, he nevertheless lives with his long-suffering wife, two adult children and a cat. It's just possible the cat is the sanest one of them all. For more information please visit his official website - http://www.nwdavies.co.uk, or find him on Facebook (nwdavies), Twitter (@nwdavies), and Instagram (nwdavies).

If you liked the stories you've just read, then check out Neil's other works: *The Demon Guardian* and *Vampire Worms*.

CHAPTER ONE

It was one of those rare mornings when Dennis Parkes woke at peace. Cautiously, he lifted his head, waiting for the quick, shadowy movements seen from the corner of his eye, the sibilant whispering filling the stale air of the small bedroom. There was nothing. Just still, silent darkness.

He thought of waking his wife, Swan, to share his sense of relief and happiness, but she had never heard the voices or seen the shadows move. If he woke her, she would be angry at being disturbed more than an hour before the alarm was due. It would ruin his mood. It would ruin the stillness. He eased his head back onto the pillow and lay awake, enjoying the silence, the peace.

Slowly, dawn lit up the window through the thin curtains, and birdsong twittered and whistled through the trees of nearby Ottmor Wood. If only all mornings could be like this, he would not need the medication, the therapy. It might even make his life with Swan less combative.

If only.

Wyatt Road lay quiet and sleepy on the outskirts of Anbal, a small village on the Wirral Peninsula. The commuter traffic, from Liverpool to the north and Chester to the south, bypassed Anbal on the M53 motorway. What little diverted through the narrow main street of the village itself passed the end of Wyatt Road without any thought of turning in. Wyatt Road was a dead-end. If you didn't live there and were not visiting, your only destination would be the turning circle just before the wooden stile leading to Ottmor Wood.

It was the quiet, more than anything, that had drawn Swanhild Parkes to number 20 when it came up for sale. A narrow mid-terraced house, it stood more or less equidistant between the end of the road and the wood. Built in the early 1930s, it had more-recent additions of a concrete driveway at the front, newly installed plumbing and electrics, and a narrow, but long, well-groomed garden at the back. That was eleven years ago, when she had persuaded Dennis that this should be their first family home. Now, standing at the kitchen sink, staring at the overgrown lawn, the legs of upturned plastic chairs like skeletal limbs reaching up from the long grass, she felt nothing but despair.

"It's not my fault I got made redundant," shouted Dennis from somewhere behind her. She had almost forgotten they were mid-argument. The same argument they had had almost weekly for the last three years.

"No," she said, agreeing. "But it is your fault that the grass hasn't been cut for weeks."

"You know it hurts my back."

"We can't afford to get someone in anymore," she said, striving to be both truthful and understanding. "Since you can't do it, *I'll* have to do it at the weekend."

"I'll worry if you do that. I don't want you to do that."

His voice almost whined. She hated it when he whined.

"Yes, well, there's not much choice, is there?" She turned from the sink to face her husband. "Now, I have to get to work."

"I'll move the car," said Dennis. "May as well go to the shop while I'm out."

He turned and began burrowing through the accumulated clutter under the stairs for his shoes.

Swan wanted to be even more truthful. She wanted to tell her husband that he was a morbidly obese, out-of-work man in his early forties, and that it was no wonder his back and joints hurt, given the weight they were carrying. But she knew the redundancy had hurt him badly, destroyed his confidence, shoved him into depression, and that the weight gain was almost completely due to emotional eating since then. He was not currently fit for work, mentally or physically. She wanted to tell him these things, but she knew it would just deepen his depression and worsen an already terrible self-image. He needed to know she supported him, still loved him, despite all that had happened.

Dennis had found his shoes and, with some difficulty, put them on. Breathing heavily, he led the way out of the front door. Swan shrugged on her one and only coat and followed.

Dennis reversed his old Peugeot 405 out of the narrow driveway and waited, the engine idling. He felt comfortable in the car, able to relax, away from whispered voices, away from Swan. Alone. It had been bought for the long drive to his last place of work, and he held on to it stubbornly after the redundancy. Big and impractical it might be, given how little driving he now did, but it was *his*. And it was the only thing that connected him to his old life. His purposeful, *employed* life. When he hadn't felt quite so worthless. When he didn't spend days in introspection and deepening depresssion. When he felt confident his wife loved him.

Swan's Vauxhall Corsa reversed out, and the bright pink of the bodywork pulled a slight smile out of his frown. Even she agreed she bought it more for the colour than the car itself.

They waved to each other as she drove off, and Dennis waited until he saw her safely negotiate the junction at the end of the road before he put the Peugeot into gear and headed for the shops.

Just get the essentials and back home.

But did he really want to be home? There was nothing there but an empty house, another long day of watching the clock ticking slowly by, the flash of movement from the corner of his eye—and the voices.

He wanted to tell Swan, he really did. But how do you tell your wife that you hear voices in the home you share? She already thought him fat and useless, blamed him for his depression and for failing to get another job. To admit to hearing voices and seeing things would finally convince her he was completely insane. She would probably leave. He couldn't risk that.

Only two other people knew about the voices and the shadows: his local general practitioner, Dr. Banks, and his one and only friend, Travis

Newman. The only two people he had told differed in their reactions.

"It's not that unusual," Dr. Banks had said. "Particularly in someone suffering from clinical depression, like yourself."

"But what do the voices mean?" said Dennis. "Why are they mostly unintelligible? Shouldn't they be sending me messages from God or something?"

Dr. Banks smiled. "The mind is a complex thing," he said. "It can push bad and unpleasant thoughts aside if it doesn't want to deal with them. It separates them, and they become a different part of you."

"You mean like another person in my head?"

"Not quite, but another aspect of you, certainly." Dr. Banks removed his narrow-framed glasses and held them in his right hand, twisting them back and forth as he spoke. "These are things you don't want to have to cope with just now, so they're pushed into the background. And mostly, that's where they stay. But every now and then they push back, and that's where the voices are coming from."

"So it's all in my mind," said Dennis. "Does this mean I'm psychotic or something?"

Dr. Banks shook his head. "No. It's not any kind of psychosis. It's *dissociation*. Like I said, it's quite common among those suffering from depression."

Travis, on the other hand, saw things slightly differently.

"So, you hear voices. Are they always in your head, or sometimes from outside?"

They had been sitting in their local Sainsburys cafe, meeting up during Travis's lunch break from his nearby office job, and before Dennis went shopping. Talking with Travis boosted Dennis's self-confidence enough to make it round the aisles without panicking.

"Sometimes in my head, sometimes not," said Dennis, keeping his voice low. He was sure some of the old people at neighbouring tables were listening.

"I don't reckon it's anything to do with depression," said Travis, casually dismissing what Dennis had told him about the doctor's opinion. "I think it's a lot simpler than all that stuff."

"Oh yes?" said Dennis, doubtfully. As a general rule, he sided with doctors over laymen, but he always had time for Travis's thoughts on matters, however outrageous they might turn out to be. "And so what do you think it is?"

"Simple." Travis leaned closer, lowering his voice to a whisper.

"Your house is *haunted*."

Dennis managed to delay returning to the house for just over an hour, driving around, listening to the inane presenters on the equally inane radio shows. But he could not put if off forever. There were things he should be doing in the house.

He knew that Swan was right when she accused him of not doing enough. But most times, including today, the low moods and aching joints were just too much to handle, and certainly too much to allow for easy housework. Nevertheless, in an attempt to make Swan happy when she came home from work, he was determined to try.

I need to start pushing myself, he thought. *It's only fair to Swan. She's out earning the money. I have to do something here in the house so she knows I'm trying to help.*

If fear of the voices was a factor, it was one he kept deliberately in the background. Maybe, for once, if he didn't think about them, they might not be there. The quiet morning might extend into a quiet day.

Everything looked fine as he stopped in the driveway and climbed out of the car, something that was becoming increasingly difficult and painful as time went by. Even as he entered the house itself, the atmosphere was peaceful, totally lacking in the low susurration of voices he dreaded. At times like this, he could almost believe he imagined it all.

What definitely wasn't his imagination, however, was the musty, unclean smell. The smell of unwashed clothes and dusty furniture. Of carpets that hadn't been vacuumed. A smell that reminded him of old people, living on their own with no family to help. Old people who did not wash, could not clean, and wore the same clothes they had worn for the last who-knew-how-many days. It was not a smell that should exist in a house occupied by a couple in their forties. It was a smell that said no one cleaned. And that no one was him.

"Okay," he said, hanging up his fleece under the stairs. "First job of the day decided. Get rid of the smell."

He was an hour into it, wiping down the kitchen worktops and almost ready to vacuum the front room carpet when the first whispers slithered into the still, musty air.

He froze, a bottle of cleaning spray raised in one hand, the other grasping a wet paper towel, mid-wipe. The usual, sensible list ran quickly through his mind: plumbing; someone walking by outside; a nearby radio; the wind, even though there was none that day. He considered them all and discarded them. Neither was it coming from within his head. It was a voice, and the source was somewhere in the house.

He was long past the point of running from this thing. Frightened, yes, but not enough to run. As scary as they were, they had never hurt him. The voices in the house were always soft, on the edge of hearing, and always unintelligible. The movements were quick but nonthreatening, and never anywhere but in his peripheral vision. If he had to give a name to his feelings when that first voice hissed by, it would be disappointment. Disappointment that a day that had started whisper-free had become like every other day.

The voice continued, a diatribe of unknown words, and Dennis wondered briefly where this particular one was coming from. The corner of some room? Behind a half-open door? The attic? Beneath the suspended flooring? From where he stood, it came from the hallway, and he glanced quickly around the kitchen door to see, with some relief, what he had expected. Nothing.

But the voice continued. Just the one. That, at least, was something to be grateful for.

He had restarted cleaning, choosing to ignore the interruption, when he heard the first intelligible thing ever to come from the voices in the house. It froze his heart.

"Swanhild."

There could be no mistaking the sound of his wife's name, dropped into the middle of the usual nonsense.

He stood still. He listened. It came again.

"Swanhild."

The voice stopped, suddenly and completely. No echo or reverberation of sound. Just his wife's name one more time, and then silence.

He put down the cleaning spray and the paper towel and hurried out into the hall. Nothing. He stepped into the front room. It was quiet and empty. Struggling up the stairs gave out no other clues. He didn't know what he was looking for, but he wanted some explanation for hearing his wife's name. He felt the same as he had the very first time he'd heard the voices. Frightened, confused, and sick.

He was still upstairs in the bedroom when the voice began again, from downstairs. It repeated one word, over and over.

"Swanhild. Swanhild. Swanhild."

Other voices joined it, a rising mass of eerie sibilance, all repeating his wife's name, none of them in unison.

Moving as quickly as he could, almost in tears from a sense of helplessness, a feeling that he was somehow failing his wife, he went back down into the hallway. The hissing, serpent-like voices surrounded him. It was no longer a case of where they came from. They came from everywhere, even from inside his own head. Repeated and repeated, battering him unceasingly, until the name became an almost unrecognisable collection of sounds. He pressed his hands to his ears. His mouth opened, wanting to shout, to tell them all to go away, but no sound emerged. Tears squeezed from tightly shut eyes.

Perhaps I really am insane.

The voices stopped with just as much suddenness as the one voice had earlier.

The silence had a sound of its own. A background hum of nothingness.

He opened his eyes. There was movement in the corners, shadows shifting and darting. It seemed somehow more frantic than usual. And then, not on the periphery, but directly in front of him, an intense Stygian blackness bled outward from the wall. It coalesced, grew, all but blocking the kitchen door from his sight. It radiated emptiness. A hole in the air before him.

Eyes snapped open in its depths. Veined, hungry, *lustful* eyes, blazing with an internal fire, shocking in their contrast with the void they floated in.

Terror gripped Dennis's heart, and he ran, puffing and panting, from the house.

CHAPTER TWO

"Thank God you're here," said Dennis as Travis's car drew to a stop at the end of the driveway.

"I told work it was a family emergency," said Travis, stepping out. "To be honest, it wasn't clear from your call what was going on."

"It's the voices, the darkness," said Dennis, pacing back and forth, agitated.

Travis saw the movement of curtains from several other houses. People were watching. Dennis's neighbors. No one had come out of their front doors to ask him what was wrong, but they were watching nonetheless.

"We need to get you inside," he said. "I'll make some tea, and we can talk about it."

He took Dennis gently by the shoulders and guided him towards the house.

He had known Dennis a long time. They had both been in their early twenties when they first met. Dennis was starting as a trainer in the small computer firm where Travis worked in marketing. They had quickly become friends through a shared appreciation of European horror movies and the kung fu films of Hong Kong. More importantly, he had the address of a mail order company that sold uncut versions on VHS. They had bonded immediately. When the computer firm folded, they lost touch, only to reconnect almost a year later, working for different companies out of the same multi-story building on the outskirts of Manchester. It was a coincidence they took as fate, and they had never lost touch since. Not even as Travis continued into graphic design work with another company and Dennis moved to a local newspaper on the far side of Liverpool, managing their computers.

That was the company that had made Dennis redundant just over three years ago. Travis had watched his friend go downhill since.

As they neared the front door, Dennis resisted and pulled away. "No," he said. "Not until you know what's in there."

"You've told me all about the voices numerous times," said Travis. "And the things you see moving from the corner of your eye. What's so different this time?"

Dennis lowered his voice and leaned in towards Travis. There was a look of barely restrained panic in his eyes. "I saw something right in front of me. Not out the corner of my eye, but right in front," said Dennis. "And I know what they want. They want Swan!"

Swan stared blankly at her coffee. It swirled from the illicit spoonful of sugar she had stirred in just seconds before. Today she needed it sweet.

"Is it really that bad?" Piers Boyson stepped into the tiny kitchen, squeezing past Swan in a way that could have been awkward except for one thing. Piers's boyfriend would not be amused.

"Sometimes." Swan smiled. "How's Davin getting on in his new job?"

"Fine." Piers searched the cupboards for his box of Green Tea, finding it tucked away at the back. "And we can finally save for the wedding."

"I expect an invite."

"Of course."

As he waited for the kettle to boil, Piers looked to Swan, still staring morosely into her drink.

"Speaking of marriages," he said. "How's Dennis doing?"

Swan looked up and forced a smile. "Same as always."

"So, things not good between you two then?"

"Is it that obvious?" Swan sighed. "He just doesn't seem to try anymore. When we met, we seemed to enjoy the same kind of things, but now..."

"I'm sure he's finding the whole thing difficult, too," said Piers. "The redundancy hit both of you hard."

Swan nodded, never taking her eye off the coffee, the swirl gradually slowing until it slid to a graceful stop.

"I just get fed up sometimes," she said quietly. "I feel down."

Leaving his green tea to brew, Piers placed a gentle hand on Swan's shoulder.

"You should come out with Davin and me," he said. "Just for a few drinks after work. Something to take your mind off things for a while."

"That's kind of you, but I have to get straight home." Swan smiled again, slightly broader this time. "Some time soon though, yes?"

Piers's attention was drawn by a passing doctor. Tall, muscular, perfect hair and teeth. Almost a caricature of *the young doctor*. He even had the stethoscope around his neck.

"Doctor Mayson," whispered Piers. "Now there's something to take your mind off your troubles."

Swan glanced at the passing doctor and blushed. "I would never do that," she said.

Piers smiled. "I would."

"We should get back to work," said Swan, laughing, feeling better than she had. "There's probably patients waiting."

As they left the kitchen, Swan's eyes lingered on the retreating back of Dr. Mayson.

Dennis let Travis lead the way. He knew it was a cowardly thing to do, but he was too frightened of what he might see. It was all he could do to hide behind his friend and not run away again. He had not felt such fear since, as a small child, he would wake from nightmares, screaming and crying. Even then, his father told him he was a coward. Only his mother seemed sympathetic.

The child that never quite grew up inside him wished his mother were alive and with him now.

"What am I meant to be looking for exactly?" said Travis as he opened the door and stepped into the hallway. "Oh my God!"

"What?" Dennis almost turned and fled, panic rising within. "What do you see? What's there?"

"Your house is such a mess!" said Travis, turning and grinning.

Dennis almost punched him, only slowly seeing the funny side and forcing a smile. He should have known better than to think Travis could keep his sense of humor in check.

"There's nothing there, Dennis," said Travis seriously. "At least, nothing I can see out of the ordinary."

Dennis looked past his friend to see his hallway. It was as if nothing had happened.

"I saw something coming out of that wall," he said. "I know it sounds ridiculous, but I saw it."

"What did it look like?" Travis ran his fingers over the wall indicated by Dennis. It was solid. "Was it a person?"

"I…I don't know." Dennis pinched the bridge of his nose between thumb and forefinger. He could feel a headache growing. "It was just a shape. Black. And then the eyes."

"Eyes?"

"This pair of eyes opened up and looked at me from the blackness." Dennis sighed. "That's when I ran."

Travis placed a hand on Dennis's shoulder. "Don't worry about it, mate. If I'd seen that, I'd have run, too." He smiled. "Close the door and I'll make us a cup of tea."

Dennis watched Travis head into the kitchen, then, as suggested, turned to close the front door.

Did I really see that thing? Or am I truly going mad?

He was not sure how to answer. When he ran, he had no doubt about what he saw. Now, he wondered whether he had overreacted to something that might have a perfectly reasonable explanation. Not that he could think of one at that moment.

As he turned to follow Travis into the kitchen, the house breathed out in one long breath.

"Sssswwwwwaaaaannnnhhiiillllddd."

Swan's right leg was hooked over the back of the driver's seat. Her left foot brushed the low roof with each thrust, her lover's arm hooked behind the knee, keeping it high. At first, she wondered how he could be in any way comfortable, squeezed between the front seats and the back. But then he began to move, and she no longer cared. He kissed her mouth, her cheek, her neck. Breathed heavily into her tangled hair. Lifted himself up on muscular arms and looked down on her nakedness, smiling, sweating.

She had no idea how he was at medicine, but there was no doubting that Dr. Mayson was a good fuck.

CHAPTER THREE

The world through the windscreen melted as heavy raindrops distorted Swan's vision.

What have I just done?

She sat alone in her car. Dr. Mayson—she didn't even know his first name—had not long driven off home. Back to his wife and children. She knew he had children because afterwards he had shown her their pictures. Jen and Simon. He told her his children's names, but never his own. What kind of screwed morality was that?

Not that I'm in any position to comment on another's morality.

She could smell the sex they'd had. It tainted the air. Rain spat in her face as she let down the driver's window. It speckled the plastic of the dashboard, but at least it cleared the air a little.

I suppose I should be grateful he had condoms with him.

But then again…

He had condoms with him! Guess I'm not the first.

The dashboard clock, lending a spectral light to a rapidly darkening interior, told its own story of her infidelity. As did her iPhone, which was in her bag and turned off. The phone she could explain, using the poor-to-no reception in the hospital as an excuse for being out of touch. But the time… Almost an hour and a half late. Dennis would not be happy.

Dennis!

The first tears came slowly, meandering over her cheeks with the slightest of tickling sensations.

Trying to understand why she'd done it seemed a fruitless expenditure of energy. Words like *urge*, *uncontrollable*, and *desperate* were trivial and incomplete. It had been a *collection* of urges. She *had* been out of control. And she and Dennis had hardly been intimate since Dennis's self-image worsened almost two years ago. But it was more than that. She had felt not only out of control, but out of her body. Pushed aside by *something*. And it was that *something* that had followed Dr. Mayson to this secluded spot. That *something* that engaged energetically in quick, almost violent, sex with a near stranger in the back of her car.

She started the engine. There seemed little point in analysing further. It was the first time she had been unfaithful to Dennis. But she could not rid herself of the feeling that it might not be the last. The *something* could return at any time, and that thought brought both excitement and sickness to her stomach.

Windscreen wipers restored solidity to the world outside as she drove off, leaving the driver's window down, the rain mixing with her tears.

"Where is she?"

Dennis sat forward in his armchair, eyes flitting between the clock, Travis relaxing on the couch, and SpongeBob on the TV. Travis had chosen the channel. It was something that would normally make both of them laugh. Dennis did not feel like laughing today.

"She'll be along soon," said Travis, smiling at the TV. "Just try and relax. Watch some SpongeBob. Personally, I find I empathize more with Patrick. What do you think?"

Dennis, not even conscious of the attempt to draw him into light-hearted conversation, looked again at the clock.

"Even working late, she'd normally be home by now. Do you think she's okay?"

"She's fine," said Travis, struggling to keep the smile on his face. He saw his role, for now, as keeping Dennis on the right side of sanity until Swan got home. He just hoped *she* could do a better job than he was doing.

"What if the voices start again?" said Dennis, gently rocking back and forth. "What if that thing comes back out of the wall? What if she's been in some kind of accident?"

The changes in the focus of Dennis's anxiety almost caught Travis out. When Dennis started on about the voices or the manifestation he was convinced he'd experienced, Travis more or less switched off. There was nothing he could say. But worrying about Swan being in an accident was something he could not ignore. That was a *real* worry, and one that had crossed his mind, too. Not that he would ever admit that to Dennis.

"She hasn't been in any accident," he said, hoping he sounded convincing. "She's just late. We've all been late in our time. Even you, Dennis."

Dennis said nothing, but his silence was tense as he clenched and unclenched his fists, rocking back and forth on the edge of the chair.

When they heard the key turn in the front door, it was difficult to say which of them was more relieved.

Swan perched on the edge of Dennis's chair. He grasped her hand in his fist, unwilling to let go.

"Why didn't you tell me about the voices, Dennis?" She wanted desperately to go upstairs and change, have a shower, wash away every trace of Dr. Mayson, but Dennis would not let her out of his sight.

"I was worried you'd think I'd finally cracked," said Dennis, smiling up at her nervously. "I thought with Dr. Banks's help, and Travis's, I'd get it sorted out without you ever having to know."

"And *you* didn't think to tell me?" This was directed at Travis, who still sat across the room.

"Dennis didn't want me to."

Swan shifted slightly on the arm of the chair. She was conscious of the way her skirt rode up above her knees. She kept her legs very deliberately pressed together. It was not that she was shy around Travis, but she hadn't wanted to put her panties back on after using them to wipe herself in the car earlier. She had discarded them in a ditch near the site of her liaison with Dr. Mayson.

"I've known you almost as long as I've known Dennis," she said. "You should have told me."

"It was different this time, Swan," said Travis. "Dennis has never called me out of work before, not because of the voices. He was genuinely terrified of coming back into the house alone."

She tightened her grip on Dennis's hand.

"I'd never seen anything right in front of me before," said Dennis quietly.

"It must have been scary," said Swan. "You did the right thing, calling Travis."

"I would have called you, but I know your phone doesn't work well in the hospital. And you couldn't just leave patients sitting there, waiting to see you."

"Maybe it's stress?" said Swan. "Between how depressed you are, then hearing the voices again. Things can get confused with shadows, light, even cars passing outside the window."

"Maybe," said Dennis, but it was obvious to Swan that he did not believe that. If *she* had seen it, she probably wouldn't believe all the usual, rational explanations either.

"There is one other thing," said Dennis. "I wasn't sure whether to tell you."

"Tell me, Dennis," said Swan. "Really, you can tell me anything. You know that."

With only a slight hesitation, Dennis continued. "After Travis was here and we came back inside, I heard the voices again."

Swan smiled. "Well, I don't suppose they're just going to disappear like that, even with someone else in the house."

"No, it's not that," said Dennis. "It's what they said. What they were saying before the thing appeared. Normally I can't make it out, but this time they were saying your name. Swanhild."

"*My* name?"

"Very clearly. They kept saying your name, over and over."

Swan said nothing, a sudden tightening of her stomach making her feel sick. She had no proof, but she felt strangely certain that Dennis was hearing these voices at the same time she was with Dr. Mayson. She didn't believe in ghosts and all that supernatural crap, but she did wonder if Dennis's subconscious somehow knew what she was doing. Telepathy and such had been investigated by science, hadn't it? Weren't there some scientists who claimed it was real? Hadn't the Americans done something with it during the war, or the Cold War, or whenever? She didn't believe in ghosts, but she was willing to believe in the untapped power of the human mind.

If Dennis's subconscious knew what I was doing, how long before it gets to his conscious thoughts? Was it worth risking my marriage for one vaguely disappointing fuck? Why did I do it?

She became slowly aware that Travis was staring at her oddly. Was that suspicion on his face? Had he somehow guessed?

Following Dennis's revelation, one of her legs had unconsciously slipped from the arm of the chair. Her thighs had parted and her skirt ridden higher. With sudden embarrassment, she rectified the situation, but was it too late? Was that why Travis was looking at her so strangely? She needed a change of clothes. She needed a shower. Most of all, she needed to throw up to try and ease the churning of her insides.

Neil Davies

VAMPIRE WORMS

Chapter One

They floated in on the breeze, light as gossamer, translucent in the sun hanging low and hazy over the Cheshire fields. No one noticed them. Rippling, almost invisible, they snaked over the clock tower, the church spire, the homes, and the workplaces of Taupmere, and no one knew they had arrived.

Until people began to die.

Chapter Two

Paul Walker made his tea and toast as quietly as he could, wincing at the bubbling of the kettle and the inordinately loud popping of the toaster. He didn't want to wake his sister. If he did, she would undoubtedly want him to make her breakfast, and he really didn't have the time or inclination.

He buttered the toast and ate it standing at the marble-effect kitchen unit. A round table and two chairs sat no more than three feet behind him, but he preferred to eat and drink on his feet. Dirty dishes were stacked unevenly in the sink and on the draining board. He had considered putting on the dishwasher, but the noise would wake Janet, and he had already decided he didn't want to do that.

The house was old and small, built of brick and local stone. A cottage, if you discarded the romantic, flower-framed image of the fairy tales, sitting mid-terrace in a residential suburb of Taupmere. It was barely big enough for the two of them, and yet it had once been home to both them and their parents. Now, only Paul and his sister remained.

He drank half of his tea and then, glancing at the clock, poured the rest away down the side of the dishes in the sink. It had gone on 6:00 a.m., and he needed to get moving. But before he left, he loaded the coffee machine and set it going. Janet would need her coffee when she finally woke.

Silvery slug trails disrupted the regular pattern of the hall carpet, and he sighed. Overnight, the slugs had left swirling, crisscrossing patterns that, were they anything but slime, might have been appealing. Instead, they just reminded him he needed to vacuum when he got home that evening. He could ask Janet, but it didn't seem worth the waste of breath.

Grabbing his jacket from the coat hooks under the stairs, he eased open the front door and slipped out. It was, on the whole, a good start to the day.

* * *

Janet Walker woke as the front door closed. Was it that time already?

Had she woken before Paul left, she would have asked him to make breakfast of some sort. If she thought she could keep it down. Eating was a challenge the *morning after*. Cooking was out of the question.

She shuffled out of her bedroom and down the hall to the kitchen, unknowingly breaking the pattern of slug slime with her bare feet. Her nose twitched at the smell of coffee. Paul was thoughtful like that. Knew she would need coffee when she finally faced the daylight.

Each small movement of her head pulsed pain behind her eyes, and she felt ready to allow last night's pizza to see the world again. Why did she drink so much? Why did she end up eating pizza? She didn't even like pizza! Then she remembered. It was all they had in the fridge, and she needed to eat something, anything, after her night with the bottle.

Coffee was the only thing she could face. A mug of coffee, and then some fresh air, might just blow the alcohol-dipped cobwebs away.

Chapter Three

They floated in over the buildings, silent and unseen. At first glance, it might have seemed they flew randomly, but there was a pattern, a twisting, sweeping, searching pattern.

Local businessman Ed Malone was one of the first to notice them. As he unlocked the door to Taupmere Wholesalers, he looked up and saw the one dropping out of the sky towards him.

Chapter Four

Paul picked up his unofficial work colleague two corners away from home.

Chris Benson didn't work for the company, but he was Paul's oldest friend and currently unemployed. Some days he helped Paul out for a little cash on the side.

"Did you get out without waking the old spinster?" Chris smiled as he climbed up into the van's passenger seat.

"I don't think thirty-four really classifies as old," said Paul, pulling back out onto the deserted street.

"Older than us," said Chris. "Same thing."

"Yes, I got out without waking her."

"I'm proud of you."

Chris noticed a well-thumbed paperback on the dashboard and, reaching forward, picked it up. "*Dracula*," he said. "Really? Again?"

"It's a classic," said Paul, snapping. "I like to re-read classics."

"I'm just messing with you," said Chris, shaking his head at the obvious annoyance in his friend's voice. "You sound tired. You know, you can't keep on looking after the house and your sister on your own. It'll kill you."

"When our parents died, I took on the responsibility," said Paul. "Nothing's changed."

"Janet's the oldest—"

"She's not capable!" interrupted Paul, snapping again.

Chris paused, giving Paul time to cool down. He was concerned, and this was not the first time this particular discussion had caused some tension between them. But he hoped Paul would see sense eventually. "I like Janet," he said. "And I know she has problems. But she needs to do her fair share."

"Are you going to help me with today's list?" said Paul. "Or should I just let you out here?"

Chris sighed. As always, Paul did not want to be drawn into a serious discussion about his sister. She was draining every last drop of energy from him, and yet he wouldn't talk about it. It was frustrating, but Chris knew his friend well enough to know when to back off. "When's the first pickup?" he said, putting *Dracula* back on the dashboard and glancing at the inlaid clock. 6:33 a.m.

"First pickup, 7:00 a.m.," said Paul. "We'll be early."

"Time for a break then." Chris hunkered down in the seat and closed his eyes. "Wake me when you need me. These early starts tire me out."

* * *

Paul pulled the delivery van to the curb and let the engine idle. He double-checked his paperwork. *Pickup at 7:00 a.m., Taupmere Wholesalers.*

Killing the engine, he unclicked his seatbelt and grabbed *Dracula* from the dashboard. As long as he made his pickups and deliveries on time, he could take a few minutes to catch up on his reading. The downside of the job was the pay. But money wasn't the driving force behind Paul Walker. Job satisfaction and the avoidance of too much stress were much higher priorities.

Janet did not agree. "We need more money. Why can't you get a better job? A higher paying job! You're not stupid; you're just lazy!"

He had heard the words time and again, to the point where they barely registered as they were growled at him. He *knew* they needed more money, but he didn't see why he should be the one to change his job. Janet claimed to be an artist, a painter, but she hadn't sold anything in years. She was eight years older than him, but he felt the more mature of the two.

Pushing his bitterness to the background, determined it would not spoil the start of his day, he opened *Dracula* at the scrap of paper that acted as a bookmark. He loved the Gothic, the vampire, in fiction. His collection, overflowing the small bookcase in his bedroom, ranged from the classics of Sheridan Le Fanu and Bram Stoker to more recent interpretations, like Anne Rice and Brian Lumley. He loved them all. Except for the recent trend of teenage vampires with more angst than bite.

He glanced down at his black t-shirt, black trousers, black shoes. He caught sight of his close-cropped black hair in the rearview mirror and raised thick eyebrows in amusement. If only he had the cape and teeth to match.

Glancing momentarily towards Chris, who had begun to gently snore, he settled himself in the warmth of the morning sun coming through the windscreen and began to read. Time for a few pages. Time to immerse himself.

He jumped as something hit the car with a loud *thump,* leaving a greasy smear as it slid off the windscreen. It happened too fast for him to catch anything but the briefest glimpse, but he had the impression of something long and near transparent.

"Did you see that?" he said, turning to Chris. But Chris continued to snore, undisturbed by the noise.

Paul leaned forward, but he could see no sign of whatever had hit the windscreen. For a moment, he considered climbing out of the van and looking around, but his curiosity was not that strong, and he didn't want to waste good reading time. Instead, he pumped the washers, flicked the wipers, and managed to clear most of the smear from the glass.

Satisfying himself that it probably fell from a nearby tree, some strange piece of foliage, like sticky weed or something, he returned to Transylvania and Jonathan Harker.

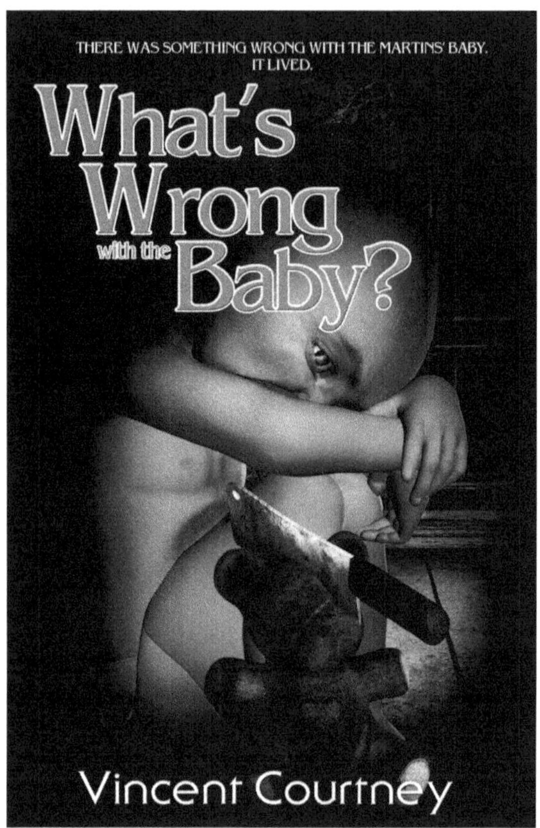

THE FEAR IS GROWING

From the moment he saw the ancient castle rising out of the picturesque Scottish countryside, filmmaker Dan Martin knew he'd found the ideal location for his vampire horror movie. And nothing could make him leave. Not the eerie legends of soul-stealing beasts of the night...nor a bizarre series of freak accidents. Not even his pregnant wife's tragic miscarriage.

THE TERROR IS BORN

Except that now there is another fetus growing in Vicki's womb. But little Darian is not going to be a normal baby. The Martins' adopted ten-year-old son Marty will soon find that out. In fact, Marty will soon know exactly what his new brother really is.

Midnight.

The Witching Hour.

But the creatures of darkness are not
confined to the shadows of the night.
Lonely stretches of highways…
Bustling college campuses…
Quiet suburban neighborhoods…
Pricey, upscale day spas…
They're everywhere.

Earl and Dale, a pair of burly truckers,
seem to be drawn to those that dwell in the darkness.
Monster hunters by default, they
confront the evil fearlessly—and with just a bit of humor.
Vampires, werewolves, half-human spider demons,
and those that prey on the innocent…
All will realize they've met their match
when they go head to head with…

The Midnight Men

Shrouded in Mystery

The locals call it *Isla de los Perdidos.*
Island of the Lost.
According to the legends, those who venture onto the shores of
this cursed island never return.

Abandoned

Valarie DeNola and her sister Julie have chosen to ignore the
legends and the warnings. They have been selected to lead a team
of explorers to the island to discover the mystery surrounding it.
But once ashore, they become cut off from the outside world, and
what they discover is something they could never have prepared
for.

Inhabited by Death

Now they must fight against an unknown presence that is picking
them off one by one. No one can be trusted, and when even nature
rises up against them, all seems lost. Their one hope is the
extraction team they know is coming.

But will any of them survive to see it arrive?